DOOR
and other twisted tales

Catherine McCarthy

To Dad, with apologies for the occasional profanities used by my characters. I had no influence over the way they spoke to me.

Contents

Introduction

Readers often ask where a writer's ideas for a book stem from, so I thought I'd take a few moments to share with you how Door and other twisted tales came about...

The idea for the first story – *Door* – was sprung during a long car journey. The road we travelled passed by a barren wasteland, where stood a derelict building surrounded by barbed wire fencing. The location brought to mind a secret, government complex and for the rest of the journey I began to wonder what tales might be hidden behind its benign but sturdy looking door – and it all started from there really.

Having written *Door*, I fell in love with the notion of our world having been visited by supernatural forces – in all sorts of locations down through time – resulting in the death, disappearance or destruction of people and places.

Thus the collection grew and grew, resulting in the book you are about to read.

I hope you enjoy.

Door

Day One. 8:24a.m.

Fingers fumbling, John turns the key in the heavy gauge lock and heaves open the weighty, anodized gate. The protesting squeal of metal sets his teeth on edge. Re-entering his '94 Ford pick-up, he proceeds slowly along the rutted track ahead to Gate 2.

Handbrake on, back out the truck, re-lock gate. This procedure repeated another twice - as instructed **in bold** in the job manual - before his tyres eventually churn their way along the long gravel track ahead, towards the building...

Red fob for all keys to building. Remembers this as he switches from blue fob. No other vehicles. (As expected.) Total silence! (Rather surprising, considering not a quarter mile back he had driven through forest track – would have expected birdsong at very least.) Or is there a distant whir of machinery? Difficult to ascertain, as tinnitus is ever-present issue of late.

Main door re-locked behind him once inside. (Slight concern regarding fire-risk.) Still, need to eradicate all negative thoughts as part of Fresh Start!

A few paces along the featureless corridor and opens door marked **Office**. Windowless. Feels about for light switch.

Walls – elephant grey, desk – dove grey, smooth tiled floor – charcoal grey.

Silence. Complete and utter silence!

John flicks the row of power points along wall to left and the computer and row of dials whirr into life.

Over the past week, he has read, re-read and done his best to digest the manual that had been hand-delivered through his letter box at 5:30a.m. the previous Wednesday, just a day after the telephone interview. The thud of its delivery as it had hit the tiled floor of the hallway had woken him from a fitful sleep.

Still, best be certain. Spreads manual open in front of him, (no room for error) and begins to follow the instructions in minute detail, nervously watching the pressure needles on the dials to his right first waver, then gradually climb to **green zone** before steadying themselves. He locks them down, breathing a sigh of relief. Piece of piss he thinks, smiling for the first time that morning.

*

The telephone interview had gone well. The interviewer's controlled and steady voice had explained that everything he would need in order to carry out the job would be detailed in *the manual*, and that as long as he followed the instructions *to the letter*, the job would be *straight forward and undemanding*.

'Feel free to read, listen to music – whatever you want to help pass the time,' the faceless voice had said at the other end of the line. 'As long as the dials remain in the green zone that's pretty much it.'

John had only asked one question – 'When would you like me to start?' And here he was, earning a modest but fair income for pressing a few switches and keeping an eye on a some dials for eight hours, five days a week.

An hour or so later, John cracks his knuckles and returns to the corridor to locate the toilet and kitchen area. 'Just make sure you leave the dials unattended for no longer than fifteen minutes at a time,' the interviewer had instructed. 'This will mean you having to forego a proper lunch break, but once they're on green it's vital you keep a close eye on them.'

Plenty of time to go to the toilet, grab a coffee then.

Shit! Promised to switch to green tea, John reminds

4

himself.

The manual had reinforced the '**DO NOT LEAVE THE MACHINE FOR LONGER THAN 15 MINUTES!**' instruction in bold, red and capitalized font, so John carefully notes the exact time as he seeks out the kitchen – 9:22a.m.

Kitchen is located next to the door marked **Office** and is marked **Facilities**. The narrow, galley room - also windowless - with a stainless steel sink unit, a kettle and a further door to a toilet and hand basin, consists of the same flooring and grey laminated worktop as **Office**. Black coffee in hand, (green tea tomorrow - today he needs the caffeine to calm his nerves) John returns to **Office**.

Day Two. 11:23a.m.

Second black coffee of the morning in hand, John is about to re-enter **Office** when, having checked his watch, he notes that there are nine minutes remaining before dial check is necessary. Suddenly feeling the urge to stretch his legs, he places the mug on the floor, turns right and proceeds down the long, ash-grey corridor which stretches in front of him. Vision and sense of balance suggests that the corridor slopes away at a gradient of approximately 1 in 20.

Ninety paces (nice, even number) it takes to reach the end, where stands a solid, gunmetal-grey door. No handle, no lock, no keyhole. Slightly peculiar John thinks, glancing at watch before re-pacing the corridor to the door marked **Office**.

Ninety seven paces due to gradient. (Slightly disconcerting. Odd number. Pattern less.) Six minutes, twenty eight seconds remaining before dial check required. John checks anyway. Needles safely in green.

Day Three. 2:43p.m.

Green tea (first of day) in right hand, John re-traces corridor to **Door**. Places left palm flat against **Door** and quickly retracts. Colder than anticipated! On inspecting the heavy hinges, discovers approximately 4mm of brown rust; notes first sign of colour inside building! Smiles to self. Retraces footsteps to door marked **Office** taking slightly smaller steps.

One hundred paces! (Feels calmer. Nice even number!) Places tea on desk and decides to visit toilet before drinking. Returns with 2.5 minutes to dial check remaining. 'It's all good man!' Reads second book of week to end – H.P. Lovecraft's The Call of Cthulhu.

Day Nine. 9:29a.m.

Slept badly, Knackered this morning! Probably due to change in diet John assumes, as it is his fifth day without caffeine or alcohol. Plugs in portable radio brought from home. (Tinnitus has been major issue all week, probably made worse by overwhelming silence in building.)

10:12a.m. Sudden stomach cramps send John rushing to toilet. (Bloody green tea!)

10:17a.m. John returns to **Office**, black coffee in hand to chorus of *Ghost in my House* playing on the radio.

11:32a.m. Caffeine has kicked in and John feels the need for some exercise. Ninety paces to **Door** – both hands flat against it, (having rubbed them briskly together first in anticipation of cold) feet together, approximately one metre away. Voice in head, Give me twenty!

One hundred (slightly small) paces back to **Office**. Repeats procedure five times. Returns to desk with just twenty eight seconds to spare. Needle on dial three

6

descending towards border of red zone! Fingers trembling, heart racing, adjusts dial back to green! Cold, clammy sweat spreading. (Caffeine, exercise or needle?) John spends remainder of morning at desk, radio playing quietly in background.

Three songs in a row and he's liked none of them. Decides to wait until he's heard three in a row which he does like before allowing himself to return to **Facilities** to get lunch.

Day Fifteen. 9:02a.m.

Mobile in hand, John walks the circumference of the entire grounds of the compound in an attempt to get a signal. He's not surprised there's no signal inside the building, nor is there a land-line, but he's annoyed to discover no trace of a signal outside. How is he supposed to phone the bloody rental agency to report the blocked sink when they only open Monday to Friday 9:00a.m. to 5:00p.m?

Approximately ninety six paces towards the far end of the brick building, he expects to find external side of **Door**.

Nothing! Strange – must either lead to an internal room then or must have been bricked up, John decides. Still, better get that damned computer going!

Day Twenty Two. 3:16p.m.

Fifth round of pacing and **Door** presses completed, John makes his final ascent back to **Office**... Ninety nine, a hundred, a hundred and one. Fuck it! How can that be? He is certain that the length of his stride is exactly the same as on previous occasions. John glances at his watch, desperate to retrace the corridor to check – not enough fucking time!

3:48p.m. Eighty seven, eighty eight, eighty nine...

Bollocks! There's no way he's going to reach **Door** with just one pace. John glances down at his feet, as if they are to blame. He checks he's put on his usual work shoes. Yes. What the fuck does it matter? You must have altered your length of stride! He tries to convince himself, but the extra metre of ash-grey floor tiles smirks silently.

Turning around and ensuring both heels are touching **Door** he inhales deeply and prepares for the slight gradient ahead...

Ninety eight, ninety nine, one hundred, one hundred and fucking one!

Three more attempts and it's still fucking ninety one down and a hundred and one back! And *Radio Two* in **Office** is playing Supertramp's *Dreamer* mockingly.

Day Thirty. 9:02a.m.
Fresh start! Today's the day! John decides. No more coffee, no more alcohol, no more counting steps, or reading too much into song lyrics. Last night, Joanne had rung out of the blue. They'd talked for ages and even discussed the possibility of going on a holiday together to see if they could make it work.

11:23a.m. Determines to try and incorporate some exercise into his breaks. Getting a little flabby lately – what if that holiday comes off? Jogs down corridor. (Less chance of counting the number of steps.) Holds out both hands to slow his self propulsion as he reaches **Door**.

BANG!!! The loud, metallic thud reverberates through his head before vibrating down his arms and torso where it proceeds to echo around the building. Heart races at the sudden exertion as well as the volume. Could the extra speed enable him to repeat the exercise sequence six times instead of the usual five within fifteen minutes?

John returns to **Office** sweating and panting but enjoys

feeling the adrenalin coasting through his veins.

2:05p.m. Feet up and crossed one over the other on the desk in front of him reading Stephen King's *Dreamcatcher*. (Mother's warning voice in head telling him not to cross feet as can cause circulatory problems – rife on her side of family!) What the hell? Gotta die sometime! Tweedy, grey fabric chair wheeled far enough from desk to allow negating of posture rule, John suddenly stops reading mid sentence.

Quickly dons coat, exits the building, locks it securely and races along the external wall to where he is sure **Door** must meet the outside. No! He wasn't mistaken on the previous occasion, there is no external **Door**.

But if **Door** is bricked up, how the hell did it make such an echo from the inside when he banged it? Will need to measure the internal and external dimensions of the building to be certain.

Returning to **Office**, he quickly scribbles a note to self to bring his tape measure to work and places the note in his lunch box.

Day Thirty One. 8:25a.m.

John arrives especially early, before it is necessary to switch on the power, just in case the measuring process takes longer than fifteen minutes. Checks his measurements three times and just knows!

He can't be wrong! Then how the fuck did it make such an echo?

FUCKING OBVIOUS! Corridor slopes downwards! **Door** is actually underground!

Puzzle solved!

11:22a.m.

Round one of exercise. Jogs down corridor. Both hands reach out. **BANG!**

Jesus! Pain – then shock! John glances at his palms which are bright red.

Burnt!

Runs back up corridor to **Facilities** heart racing, saliva flooding mouth. Turns the cold tap on full force and plunges hands into the stream of water...

Terrified to look; he is certain he can already feel the skin blistering and peeling away from the fleshy tissue beneath.

Minutes later, cold water still running over hands and the pain gradually becomes less acute. With tip of forefinger and right thumb, John gently reaches for plug. Fills the basin with cold water and stands with both hands immersed in its depths for a further eleven minutes until he knows he has to check the dials. Pain throbs all the way from forearms to elbows. He contemplates ignoring the time. So what if the fucking needles descend to red!

Another thirty seconds pass by before sense of duty forces him to withdraw his hands from the water.

Eyes half closed. Afraid to look.

Has the pain really eased or are his hands just numb from cold? Tentatively, he dries them in a towel, expecting the pain to return.

No pain, no redness, no peeling skin.

Disbelief!

Fuck! Has he imagined it? Twenty seconds to spare and all three needles are creeping towards red. Dials quickly adjusted – safely in green.

Heart rate slowing... breathing gradually returning to normal.

John gets up and returns to **Facilities** to make a strong, black coffee.

Day Forty Two. 9:37a.m.

John listens to Pink Floyd's *The Wall* on his headphones to block out the sound. He cannot rid himself of the ever-present noises ringing in his ears and whining through his brain. He has not returned to **Door** during the past eleven days – not since the *burning* incident.

Since then, his tinnitus has amplified tenfold, manifesting in different guises: sometimes it is an almost calm whisper – like the sound of the sea in a conch shell, sometimes it is more annoying – like a radio which has de-tuned itself. At other times it is the sound of an infant choking on a string of beads. Occasionally, it takes on an even more menacing quality – a constant high-pitched dog whistle, which no human ear should ever be able to distinguish.

And Joanne never did get back to him.

10:02a.m. Pink Floyd track *Breathe* has calmed him. Really must get a grip before he puts himself at further risk. The fucking **Door** could not have burnt his hands and left no evidence! Thought about it often enough over the past eleven days and has reached the only logical conclusion, which is that as the temperature had dropped the previous night, what he had actually experienced was the cold of the metal against his palms and he had simply over-reacted. Headphones on and favourite track still playing he strides the ninety one paces towards **Door**...

Jabs quickly and lightly with left index finger, just to be sure. Nothing untoward – just cold, metal against skin. Thank fuck!

Day Forty Five. 11:26a.m.

Temperature in **Office** unbearable today! Stifling! Need some air! Probably shouldn't have downed seventh can of lager whilst watching shit on the box last night!

John goes outside and walks the perimeter of the building as far as is possible, until his progress is obstructed by the wall which joins the 12ft high security fence.

Smokes third fag of morning – drags smoke *DEEP* into lungs. Head buzzing!

Pauses at back of building and stares beyond fence towards open ground; nothing as far as the eye can see – just an area of short-bladed grass and trees in the middle distance. Can see where back of building slopes gradually downward and disappears below ground several feet beyond fence. **Door** would stand approximately ten feet on the far side of fence then? Wonders how deep below ground it exits - if indeed there is an exit - but does not possess the mathematical knowledge to work it out precisely from the internal gradient of the building. What the fuck does it matter anyway? Really must give up the fags and booze. Fucking job is so mind-numbing it's made things worse not better! Flaps shirt to waft cool air onto torso before returning to **Office** with 2.6 minutes to spare.

1:15p.m. Supermarket pre-packed plastic tub of salad for lunch in attempt to replace some vitamins lost to alcohol last night. Back outside for a walk. **Office** is so hot today! Or is it hangover? (Smirks to self.)

John paces to back of building, gulping deep breaths of fresh air as he walks. Stares blindly through fence, lost in thought.

Woke up this morning with stupid, fucking song *Disco Inferno* in head. Still fucking playing! Can't get it out, despite having radio on all morning! The fucking thing just pops back in! Must be on at least 500th replay by now!

Notices for first time that patch of grass in the approximate location of **Door** is dead - brown and withered. Weird! Maybe insufficient depth of earth to sustain life.

Day Forty Six. 7:22a.m.

Thunderstorms throughout the night and despondent drizzle this morning At least that oppressive heat has broken! Couldn't really sleep though – some real cracking thunder! Still, head is clearer today thanks to abstinence from alcohol the previous evening.

10:30a.m. First jog of day to **Door**. Feeling tired from lack of sleep. Lactic acid burn in calf muscles. Pauses for rest before return journey. Two hands placed firmly against the metal to help recover breath. Over the *burn* shit now! Reading too much fucking sci-fi! Sick of the infernal silence in this place though. Could do with some company!

What the fuck's behind this thing anyway? Why's it here?

'Hey... Door! What you hiding? Hey? Hey..? Answer me you Mother Fucker! Think you're hard do you?' (Grins at own pun.)

THWANG!

John bangs hands against **Door**. Deep metal sound reverberating throughout body and echoing around building.

THWANG! THWANG!

Enough now! That last one hurt! Still, at least it broke the god-damn silence!

Slumps to floor. Rests back against the cool metal, breathing hard. Phew!

Fucking job's driving me crazy! And to think I imagined the peace and quiet would help sort my head out! Perhaps another month – just one more pay and I'll jack it. Find something else, something with people – wearing colour! Maybe even in a building with coloured walls!

Even better – a job outdoors!

Turns and kneels in front of **Door**, placing both hands on floor to help push up from ground and the sudden, overwhelming stench hits him head-on making him gag! John pinches nose hard, and purses lips tight. Where the fuck is it coming from? Unbearable!

Has to be seeping through millimetre wide crack around

13

Door! There is no other possible source! Instant memory of himself age ten and the corpse of his beloved Mr. T., his decaying, guts-spewing pet cat, which he had eventually found mangled in a gutter having worryingly searched for him for two weeks...

The stench had pervaded both his nostrils and memory years later.

And then another memory, more recent and more poignant – that of the smell of his mother in the last two days of her life as he had held her hand and spoken to her unconscious body in the clinical, tiny hospital room nine months previous.

Yes – the smell of death was unmistakable. The vivid and sickening events flooded back as he ran, quick as his breath would allow, back to **Office**. No smell here – he's certain, and yet not really certain as the stench has attached itself to his very nostril hair!

Grabs jacket and nips straight outdoors for air. Fuck the dials! Still gagging once outside! Dry retches onto ground. Gulps fresh air greedily and blows nose forcibly into already-damp tissue located in trouser pocket.

Remembers now, that although the smell in the hospital room was undeniably one of the end of life, once he'd brought home his Mother's few belongings, the pink dressing-gown in which she'd died still smelt of her, *her* scent – not death. He'd not been able to bring himself to part with it; couldn't even wash it for months – until finally her presence had faded.

10:43 a.m. Bollocks! I'll go back in, and if I can still smell it, the fucking dials can go as fucking red as they like! I'm out o'ere!

Opens door, sniffing air inside tentatively. Nothing! Sweet F.A! Dials just on red border. Quick!

Turns dials and watches them slowly but surely return

14

to green.

Sits at desk and calms.

11:55a.m. The remainder of the morning passes by uneventfully.

John decides to stroll back to **Door**, cloth in hand to act as a gag, just in case, before eating lunch.

No smell. Nothing.

Sniffs around perimeter of **Door**. Nothing!

Back to **Office** and Googles *unidentifiable sudden smells*. Search eventually weaves him to a site on brain tumours.

Possible Symptoms include: unexplained exhaustion, headaches, fainting, seizures, unidentifiable scent, unidentifiable sounds in head etc. etc.

Shit! That's it! I have a brain tumour!

Spends remainder of day debating whether or not to ring for a G.P. appointment. Convinces himself that what he had smelt was indeed the prediction of his own death – soon to come.

Day Forty Eight. 11:23a.m.

Been feeling really down since Google search. Convinced brain tumour is now likely cause of recent weird experiences. Brought old c.d. player to office today to be able to play own choice of music rather than Radio 2's, in attempt to try to feel more positive.

Spent forty five minutes of previous evening selecting most up-beat c.d.'s within his collection. Currently playing *Boys of Summer* by Don Henley. Leans back in chair, hands behind neck, feet crossed at ankles, eyes closed...

Tries desperately to invoke favourite memory of summer long ago, aged about seventeen– the one that the lyrics in this song seem to be written about. It seems to be working. Growing calmer, breathing steadies...

Senses sudden warmth from behind– feeling of a presence. John's eyes spring open. Stomach lurches.

Someone's right behind him! He spins in his chair...
No-one!

100% certain that there actually was someone - just behind his chair - literally a whisper away! Felt its breath in his hair!

John leaps up and turns volume swiftly to zero.

Eyes scan **Office**. Nothing!

Outside to corridor.

Nothing!

Spends next five minutes searching interior of building... Nothing!

Grabs jacket and goes outside. 'Hello! Anyone there?'

Walks perimeter of grounds... Nothing! No tyre tracks on gravel other than his own. Not a sound.

Anywhere.

Stomach in knots. It's either a brain tumour or I'm definitely losing it! Shall I make that appointment? If I'm dying then do I really want to know? But maybe it's not? Maybe I just need anti-depressants? Shit! What should I do? Fails to eat lunch due to anxiety.

7:23 p.m. Back home, stomach rumbling, empty. Manages beans on toast. Trying to think positive – admits tendency towards melodrama! Maybe someone's screwing with my head?

Yes, that's it! I mean, who the fuck carries out an interview solely over the phone and then delivers the job manual through the letter box in the dark of night?

Loft ladder out – digs out spare web-cam from attic. I'll catch the fuckers tomorrow!

Day Forty Nine. 8:22a.m.

Arrives in **Office** early to set up web-cam as inconspicuously as possible.

Okay, so I'll probably see nothing today – But tonight!

5:02p.m. Drives home, breaking all speed limits, just in case *they* are doing whatever it is they do as soon as he leaves.

5:18p.m. Remotely logs in from own computer and sits, and waits, and watches...

11:29p.m. Nothing!

2:35 a.m. Nothing– Just a really bad headache from staring at the screen.

Day Fifty. 9:00a.m.

Office computer on and dials set to green. Phil Collins' *Another Day in Paradise* on radio. Flicks the sarcastic fucking thing off! Ten more days to pay cheque then I'm quitting!

9:22a.m. Into **Facilities** to make first coffee of day – de-caf.

Sudden **THWANG** echoing around building sends John out of kitchen and into corridor. Exact same noise as when he'd banged **Door**! Someone MUST be here!

Proceeds tentatively along corridor towards **Door**. Silent now.

Nothing. No-one.

Pauses at **Door**. 'Hello..?' Nothing.

Paces back to **Office**. One hundred and ten strides. Fucking corridor's grown!

Hand on **Office** door handle, about to turn and enter. Someone's in there! Definitely! C.D. is playing on full volume and he knows he hasn't even turned the fucking thing on yet! Heart racing, blood pressure pounding in ears, sweat causing glasses to slide down nose.

Should have brought my knife!

Turns handle quietly...

Opens door slowly...

Nothing! Not even the C.D.! Plug is pulled out of the wall, just where he left it last night.

Nine more days after this! 'Come on Buddy! You can do it!'

Day Fifty Four. 9:43a.m.

The noises in his head are relentless, as are the countless weird smells and even tastes. Are they real or imagined? John no longer knows nor even cares. He doesn't know how he's still functioning. How is he getting here? Or back home? He certainly can no longer remember the drive. Neither eating nor sleeping.

Just six more days...

Day Sixty. 9:01a.m.

From somewhere, some remnant of a conscious, thinking mind, he's made the decision to take what he considers to be a proactive step - the first for many days - though how he's had the energy to arrive at this decision he doesn't know.

Today there's a shovel in the back of his truck and he's going to dig...

9:15a.m. One minute remaining and he's holding out defiantly, standing in front of **Door**, instead of in front of dials. He's been out of **Office** for fourteen minutes and counting...

10, 9, 8, ... 3,2,1. John expects a siren, or at least an alarm or flashing light of some kind.

Nothing. Checks watch.

9:17a.m. Decides to return to **Office** to check. All three dials ashamedly in red zone but that's it! Returns to **Door**, convinced *it* must have something to do with the dials.

9:20a.m. Both hands placed firmly on **Door**. And he can feel it breathing, *in - out - in - out*. It's waiting for him... patiently, mocking.

And Pink Floyd's *Comfortably Numb* plays over and over as he heads outside - out of the complex - having collected shovel from truck and walked around to area of dead ground beyond fence where he's certain **Door** emerges underground.

11:25a.m. He's still digging and the pad of his left thumb is raw and bloody but *Comfortably Numb* still plays and he ignores the blood and the pain and digs... and digs.

And all the while, he can feel he is getting closer.

Door is waiting for him! It has been for the past sixty days... Just took him a while to realize it, that's all.

*

Day One. 8:45a.m.

Mike parks the car in front of the building and, as he has arrived a bit early, takes a quick stroll as far as he can around the perimeter.

Reaching the back, he gazes beyond the fence towards the distant ground. Not much to see – just some short-bladed grass and a patch of bare, freshly-dug earth. He sighs.

Once inside, he flicks the row of switches along the wall into action and the computer and row of dials whirr into life.

Hunter

Am I the hunter or am I the hunted?

I dwell alone in this wilderness. That is of my choosing, for I do not care for the company of others. My spear is my true companion for it guides me to sustenance. I carry nothing else, having no desire for worldly goods.

As I make my way throughout this world I know no fear: not when I stare into the primitive, silver eye of the wolf the moment before the kill, nor when its blood-curdling howl wakes me at night, not even when I know the pack have tracked my scent and encircle me.

I am not afraid. It is simply a matter of myself or the wolf – we both need to eat, so it merely comes down to whichever of us manages to outwit the other.

I know the pathways of these lands as well as I know the lines which cross my palm, and I fear nothing that this world holds. This is how it has been for as long as I can remember.

Yet these past days and nights I have known fear for the very first time. The very thought of it is abhorrent, and yet I have fallen hook, line and sinker into its void. I am afraid because, unlike the wolf, this *thing* is concealed from me.

It does not show itself, but I know it is there.

*

The midwinter night had closed in rapidly. The merest sliver of moonlight outwitted the blackness of the cave. The mass of clouds, which had gathered during the day, played hide and seek with the stars as they tumbled onwards in their haste to reach higher ground.

It was just as the last embers coughed and spluttered their final breath that I first noticed it. Anticipating the inevitable cold, I had wrapped the wolf's pelt about my shoulders when suddenly my bare feet, cold as stone, were swathed in an invisible blanket. My face, the skin rugged and weather-worn and thus not usually sensitive to change, scorched by an invisible torch.

I squinted into the gloom, my eyes seeing only a pattern of swirling circles of grey from behind the retina in their attempt to adjust to the sudden darkness. I saw nothing. I was blind. No movement, no shadow, nothing did I detect but black; yet I knew it was there. I was certain, without even a hint of doubt, that it stood right in front of me, for its huge presence obliterated even the sliver of moonlight, so that all before me was dark as death.

It is as I have already said; for the first time I knew fear. Despite the intense heat I shivered and cried out. Leaping swiftly to my feet I stabbed at the blackness with my spear but it was futile. No sound did it make and no movement did I feel, yet the oppressive heat stubbornly remained.

I jabbed again and again but my efforts were in vain. All I succeeded in doing was to exhaust myself. My heart raced like a trapped fox's the moment before the sharp, metallic teeth put pay to its life. The wolf's pelt had slipped to the rocky ground, but I felt no cold. My almost naked body, moist with sweat, stunk of fear. I was as one possessed!

Then, as suddenly as it had appeared, it disappeared. I did not hear it go nor did I sense any movement in the fetid night air, but the shard of moonlight returned as my companion in an otherwise desolate land. Still alert, I remained crouched, holding my spear firmly in my grasp...

Ba boom, ba boom... ba boom... ba boom.
Gradually my heart beat slowed and I shivered as the clammy sweat cooled upon my skin. Reluctant to relinquish

my weapon I searched the rocky ground about me with my free hand and found the wolf's pelt. Snatching it up I stepped backwards – one, two, three paces until I was inside the relative safety of the cave.

That night I did not sleep well. I breathed heavily into the gloom, my breath a welcome, rhythmic pulse of mist in the otherwise nothingness. I was afraid that *it* might return.

No doubt there will be those amongst you who believe that what I experienced was nothing more than the over-active imagination of the solitary. Or worse – that I was no longer in full possession of my mind; that the years of self-induced isolation had rendered me insane.

Only I know that this is not true. Not a speck of doubt remains but that it was here – watching, taunting, revelling in my terror.

Eventually fatigue overcame me and I drifted into a fitful sleep. I rarely dreamed, for I possessed a quiet mind, both by day and by night; the mind of the panther – calm, stealthy, patient. This self control was what gave me the upper hand when hunting prey.

But on this night I dreamed...

The blazing blackness had returned. It enveloped me in its heat until my skin blistered, until I could hear each layer sizzle as it roasted and until I could smell the putrid stench of my own flesh burning. I screamed with pain and my cry awoke me. I lay panting into the still, dank air of the cave.

How can blackness encompass such heat? In this world heat and light go hand in hand. They are familiar companions; cold and dark - heat and light. Then how could this *thing* which extinguished the light from my world manifest such intense heat? I considered the answer and concluded that there could be only one explanation;

this *thing* was not of my world.

It was alien to me, this reluctance to leave my cave and carry out my daily hunt, for such was my ritual; it was as natural as the certainty that day followed night. But on this day I was loath to do so. It was with trepidation that I stepped into the light of dawn, understanding that my hesitancy would be ten-fold once night returned.

I sharpened my spear on the rock until its tip glistened and then held it aloft to the sun. But it merely aroused in me a sense of foolishness, knowing that I had already used it against the *thing* and it had proved sorely lacking! Still, what else could I do? I must simply hope that I would never again encounter it.

I drank from the stream and satiated what little appetite I had with nuts and berries collected from the woods, before making my way downstream, following the tracks of the wolf pack. Having paused to examine their faeces I understood that today's journey would take me deep into the heart of the forest before I would be able to make my kill. I considered making do with a rabbit or squirrel, but this would only suffice for a day – two at most.

If I could kill a wolf then not only could I eat for a week but perhaps I might also regain some sense of mastery. Perhaps doing so might help diminish the burden of fear which currently strode beside me as an invisible and uninvited companion.

Let me assure you, there is no greater evil to man than that which the mind creates for itself, for that is all-consuming; it destroys man's wit and opens him to self-sacrifice.

My bowels were a churning pit of waste. I did not know which was worse – the fear of it returning to consume me in the intensity of its heat, or the fear of my subsequent lack of control. Many times did my mind try to reason that just because it had found me once, it did not necessarily mean it would come again. I tried to reassure myself that if it had wanted to devour me it would have done so the previous night. And yet, deep down, I knew I had become its prey. I knew that perhaps even now, as I traversed the forest in search of my own prey, it lurked in wait. It did not want to finish me quickly; instead it wished to torment me until I grew crazed.

How had I changed from a steady, logical, mortal, into a feverish, trembling wreck in the space of just one night? It did not seem possible. But I was beyond reason, for it had stolen all logic. I had once been powerful; a sniper in the forest. Now my bowels churned with cowardice.

As a gesture of courage I decided to test my will and sleep that night in the forest rather than return to the relative safety of my cave. But was this really a brave decision? Was I not more afraid of my own domain, the whereabouts of which it had certain knowledge? Was this *open to the world* environment, with only the canopy of the trees for a roof, really any more dangerous?

Out here I would most certainly be more vulnerable to attack by the wolf pack, but at least here I recognized my enemy. My nose knew its scent; my ears the howl of its call, my eyes the pattern of its prints. The only other being I thought I knew better was myself; now I doubted even that.

Night fell abruptly, as for the second night in a row the morose clouds gathered, diminishing the short daylight hours. The temperature quickly plummeted to below freezing. I had still not yet sighted the pack. They had begun the day several hours ahead of me and must, I assumed, have continued on their journey at a significant pace. This I considered unusual as wolf packs tend to rest during the day, reserving their energy for their favoured night attacks when the element of surprise means they are far more likely to overpower their victim.

25

Suddenly it dawned on me. They must have witnessed it too! Were they also fleeing its presence just as I was? All day long the forest had been unnaturally devoid of sound. As a hunter and tracker I should have noticed this sooner. Obviously I was off my guard.

I sat in silence, my back resting against a tall pine. Its companions peered down at me, swaying their heads from side to side and tutting at my lack of wit.

Since my meagre breakfast I had not taken a bite, nor had I drunk. As the last remnant of daylight faded I ambled towards the stream to quench my thirst. I reasoned that I should also eat but had brought no food, having expected to kill a wolf or at the very least, a deer. But both had concealed themselves well, even the smaller forest animals, the mice and squirrels had not shown their faces.

And now, for the first time, I also realized what it was that had contributed to the silence of the day, for the birds had not sung – not even to cry out in warning to one another. Those braver, such as the rooks, had not mocked me by cawing above my head. Indeed, I now realized that almost every trace of life seemed to have vanished from the forest. Were they in hiding or had they simply been wiped out?

Even if I had managed to make a kill I would have been reluctant to build a fire, for I feared that its light and warmth may once again attract the *thing*. Had it been the fire outside my cave the previous night which had enticed it to visit? Perhaps heat was attracted to heat and that is why it had come? Or was this simply the rambling of a mind so exhausted that it was no longer able to function logically?

For the second night in a row I slept fitfully, cold and alone, with not even the nocturnal creatures for company. That night it did not come.

At the crack of dawn I woke. I stretched my aching back and looked about.

Still. Still and silent; not even the creak of the swaying trees. The sky was a grey blanket. No break of sunlight to cheer the atmosphere; nothing but a cold, grey mist which hunkered low amidst the trees with no intention of leaving.

My empty stomach gnawed with hunger so I fed it what I could gather nearby. I sat to eat at the base of the tree and pondered what I should do next. By now I was convinced that the forest animals also knew of the *thing*, for I had never before encountered such silence.

I decided to continue my journey downstream in the knowledge that it would eventually lead to the river which would, in turn, lead to the people.

I who had sought only solace for the past twenty two years now felt the need for company! I understood that my real need was for reassurance that life continued; that it had not been entirely eradicated. But why should I care? I had never before sought human company so why now should I feel this way? I truly could not answer. It was just instinct; that of seeking the existence of life other than one's own. I simply needed to know that I was not alone in the world. Even if I had no desire for human interaction, I needed to know that somewhere out there, life endured.

Two more days and nights passed by, much as the previous one had done. Still I neither saw nor heard any signs of life, and the incessant cloud and mist continued to chill the forest air and afford me no distance vision. Without the stream to follow I would have given myself up as lost. Its burbling journey was the only sound, and I followed it in hope.

On the third day it began to widen and eventually joined the river, just as I knew it would, for I had come this way before – long ago.

That night, chilled to the bone, and having survived only on a diet of cold water and edible berries, I decided to take a chance and light a small fire. I desperately needed warmth and food. Still I had neither seen, nor heard, any trace of animal life, not even fresh droppings, but I had gathered fungi and bitter greens to cook on a stone on the fire.

I knew that having reached the river a day's journey would bring me to a little village. This, along with warm food, helped to temporarily sooth me and reignited a little hope. All the same I remained on guard, anxiously keeping watch. Having eaten and warmed myself I quickly doused the fire, my fear of attracting the *thing* still acute.

It was with great trepidation that I lay upon on my bed of leaves that night. The motionless mist clung to the trees and the silence in the air was ever present. Curled like a foetus in an attempt to retain some warmth I eventually drifted to sleep...

It was approaching the early hours when I felt it. At first, still asleep, I was momentarily comforted by its warmth. But as consciousness grew I knew it could only mean one thing; *it* had returned, just as I knew it would.

I bolted upright, eyes open, and attempted to find a point of reference in front of me. With it the blackness had returned – or was *it* the blackness? Once again its intense heat choked me until I felt as though I might suffocate. No flame, no smoke, no sound. It was simply an inferno of blackness – in front, behind, above and beneath me.

In desperation I cried out. 'Who are you? Why do you not show yourself?'

Silence answered my cry.

I knew that any attempt to fight would be useless. I was ready to face my end. With a sudden, calm sense of resignation, I slumped to the ground. Staring ahead into the nothingness I meekly allowed the ferocious heat to devour me.

No pain, no suffering and finally, no fear.

When I awoke I was perplexed, for I had not expected to awake. I sat up and gazed about. The stillness and eerie mist ensued. My heart beat rapidly and I was filled with a sense of disappointment that it had not ended. This torment, this nothingness, this waiting for it to end was worse than death.

I undressed and examined my body, expecting to see burns, but there were none. I did not understand how that could be since its heat had been so intense.

I looked about, expecting damage to the trees and foliage, but again there was none. It was then that I wondered if this were not some kind of hell. I held no belief in such things yet I could not understand how otherwise, so much heat could leave no scars.

And so it was with little enthusiasm that I continued my journey that day. I resumed the path of the river and continued to follow it for several miles, the ceaseless mist an ever-present, cloying chaperone.

Eventually it led towards the village. In the near distance I spied the simple, wooden huts. The mist allowed no longer view. As I approached I knew that I would be disappointed, that I would find no life here. The emptiness, the abandonment was inevitable. Tentatively I pushed open the door to the first hut.

My suspicions were confirmed, for it was utterly devoid of life. Whoever had once dwelt here had merely ceased to exist. No sign of struggle; no sign of panic. It did not appear that the residents had attempted to take any belongings, and yet there were no bodies. I was not surprised to find all of the other huts in a similar state.

I sat upon a crude, wooden bench, in front of the last hut, and wept. Never before had I experienced such utter hopelessness. It was one thing choosing to live out my life alone, in the knowledge that, elsewhere, others lived in their chosen way. For years I had taken for granted the sounds and sights of my companions – the birds and animals of the forest. Without realizing it they had satisfied my instinct for knowing that I was not alone.

Now there was nothing but oblivion.

I could have continued my journey and sought village after village, town after town. But however far I travelled I knew I would be met with the same nothingness.

And the cold, dank mist refused to lift.

And the invisible sun could not beat it.

If I am to be this solitary, this cold, this afraid, then I would rather it end.

I am no longer the hunter, for there is nothing to hunt.

Am I the hunted? I fear not – for it has found me twice, and instead of destroying me, has chosen to condemn me to this life.

Plague

Occasionally a door opens, just for the briefest of moments. A careless hand turns the key and already it is too late. There are those who will seize the opportunity to pass through; then there are others who will choose to remain in the comfort of the place in which they already dwell – they may not even notice the door opening!

The careless hand was a raging sandstorm which had hurtled past, defiant in its ferocity. Seeking adventure I chose to ride it but soon saw that he had done so too, only his purpose was to wreak havoc upon this new world.

I saw him – the blackest of shadows. I heard him whoop with pleasure as he sped past, his intent eager, and I smelt the decay and rot he carried with him.

He did not notice me – for to him I was of no importance. He had seized his chance to slaughter and was already intoxicated by the vapours of death…

Penne, a small, steep village in Southern France, late August 1347

'May I be spared for an hour Mother? It's so hot indoors. I should like to take a walk and collect the ripe sloe so that we may flavour the gin.'

'You may, but do not wander too far. I will need you soon to help prepare dinner.'

Eva beamed, ran towards her mother, and hugged her about the waist. She grabbed her tattered, straw hat from the peg and unhooked the large basket which hung from the rafters. She was tall enough to reach it now that she had turned sixteen.

Once outside she inhaled the sultry, summer air deeply and flapped at the front of her peasant's tunic in an attempt to ventilate her damp body. July and August had been stifling, both indoors and out. Eva preferred to bear the heat in the freedom of the countryside rather than within the confines of her village home. Six of them resided within the tiny, two-roomed hut, and at this time of year the stench from the nearby dung-heap was inescapable.

On reaching the end of the village she crossed over the little footbridge and stepped out into the countryside.

Gobi Desert, Mongolia, 1329

Eventually the storm abated, its tantrum extinguished, and it had abandoned us in the middle of the desert. From there I followed his footsteps silently, though even if I had screamed until my lungs burst he would not have acknowledged me, so engrossed in his purpose was he.

I witnessed his palpable delight in spreading the Great Pestilence, as if it were a gift from some exotic place. In all directions he travelled, not content with planning a pathway, but instead chaotically racing throughout this new world as though he feared his time here limited.

Over the years that followed not once did he cease to thrive upon the destruction left in his wake; he did not tire of it nor did he bore at the misery he caused. In fact, the greater the suffering he dealt, the greater was his joy.

I was incapable of stopping him – I was merely a witness from another time, another place, and from witnessing the first death, I bitterly regretted that I had chosen to ride the storm. I wished that I could turn back time and close the door on us both. Yet though I was impotent to prevent his sickness spreading I could not tear myself away. Wherever he went I tracked him and wept unseen and unheard beside those he made suffer. I was his imperceptible pawn, tied to him by an invisible cord. I do not know to this day what it was that held me so bound.

France, 1347

We arrived in France at the port of Marseilles by invisibly hitching a ride aboard a trading vessel. Throughout the long journey he slumbered deeply. High upon the vast, billowing sails he sat, feet crossed at the ankles and arms folded behind his sinewy neck – his guilty presence as light as a feather. He wore the sail like a hammock; even the storm did not interrupt him. He slept like a newborn: no conscience, no fear.

I did not sleep, for I could not tear my gaze from him for a second. I hoped that if I followed him long enough, studied him closely enough, I may glean some insight into how it was that he created such disease and thus such omnipotent misery. In my ignorance I believed that maybe then I could find a way to stop him.

His long repose seemed to calm him a little. From Marseilles we made our way north and west, visiting villages and towns along the way. At each he would idle now. Sometimes he would choose to observe its occupants for a short time, before inevitably exhaling his foul and unseen sickness upon them. He took wicked pleasure in studying the way in which his fetid air caused blackened swellings within the folds of their limbs, before inducing chronic fever, pain, and - after a handful of days - almost inevitable death. Some he would spare and take pleasure in watching them grieve for their loved ones as they carried the bodies to their final resting place in communal pits, crudely and hurriedly dug in the vicinity of their holy places. The prodigious number of his victims would not tolerate dignity.

In the summer heat we calmly ambled along the country lane towards Penne, as would a pair of well-fed itinerants. He appeared placated somewhat, perhaps having derived nourishment from the number of victims consumed in the previous town. An indolent expression sat upon his face and his strides were measured and more relaxed. As he strode he hummed a jolly tune.

Still we had not spoken, and still he showed no awareness of my presence. Even after all this time, when so much had passed between us, he remained unaware that he had a follower – not one who was an admirer but one who was a pursuer, for I still hoped that I may eventually effect his downfall.

It was I who noticed her first. Tendrils of long, raven hair which had escaped her bonnet now blew gently in the warm breeze as she laboured beside the foliage. Her skin seemed somewhat pale for the people of this land and bore the translucent quality of youth. Her soft lips were berry-tainted and her eyes the colour of warm honey flecked with gold. Her elegant, long fingers worked deftly at the fruit. She turned as we approached, as though sensing our presence. Even then, in those first moments, and without knowing her, I silently implored that he would spare her.

Seeing no-one on the path she turned and resumed her picking. He drew close beside her – so close that she wore him as an invisible cloak. I watched him pause and inhale deeply, in his usual preparation, as he took in her youthful figure. He observed her momentarily, holding his breath within its loathsome chamber. I reached out an invisible hand with which to pull him away. It slipped through him like an axe through a dark cloud. Indecision crossed his brow. With one hand he reached into her basket and tasted its contents, as though his decision lay in his approval or otherwise of its sweetness. The flavour pleased him and so, gesturing a small invisible nod in her direction, he turned away and continued down the lane towards the village, whistling as he went.

I hesitated, and for the first time since I had found myself in his company, chose not to pursue him.

This chance encounter was to be the turning point in my

obsessive journey. With instant recognition I knew that I could not allow this beauty, this maiden in her prime, to return home to face the whim of his temper. Nor would I risk one so innocent bearing witness to his offensive deeds. If I could only save one soul from his heinous crimes then my coming here would have been purposeful. I convinced myself then that the salvation of one was better than none.

Eva, (I was to discover much later that this was her name) drew herself up straight and stretched. Her basket was full to overflowing with ripe, purple berries. She smiled to herself, satisfied with the fruits of her handiwork, and immediately turned back in the direction of the village.

I panicked. If I were to save her then I would need to act quickly. Being so engrossed by her youthful beauty I had not yet devised a plan. I knew I was powerful – no not in the same way he was, but I had my own gifts. I focussed hard and fixed my gaze on her retreating form...

Eva stopped in her tracks. For a moment she appeared confused but soon turned on her heels and began to walk blindly towards me, away from the village. I breathed a sigh of relief.

I followed her, a pace or two behind, as she walked. She carried the basket in the crook of her right elbow. We continued in this way for a mile or so. She did not seem perturbed by her sudden change of plan; nor did she appear to notice the weight of the vessel on her slender arm. I was confident that my charm was working – at least for the present. However, I knew that if I were to spare her from him entirely I must keep her from returning home for quite some time, for lately he and I had been spending several weeks as unseen hosts in villages such as hers, choosing not to move on until he was satisfied that his evil deeds had wrought as much misery as possible upon its inhabitants.

Presently I affected a weariness upon her step. She

moved away from the track and sat down to rest in the warm grass at the foot of an old oak. Within moments she lowered her basket to the ground and curled on her side, adjusting her fatigued body into a comfortable position. The lichen was her pillow; the grass her soft blanket. I sat at a little distance and studied her. She appeared peaceful. In slumber her delicate features wore the unburdened expression of a child. Even the butterflies of the summer meadow visited to acknowledge her beauty.

As I watched I myself grew weary; the endurance of all the suffering I had witnessed on my journey suddenly rendered me exhausted.

It was Eva who woke first. Deep in sleep I became aware of a sudden movement and heard a small gasp as she bolted upright. Leaping to my feet I looked about, but there was little to see with only the moon to light the scene. The barn owl screeched in sympathy as she called out in fear, 'Maman!' but none other than I heard.

I held my head in my hands and considered what I must do next. It was not my intention to frighten her; indeed, it was fear and pain from which I sought to spare her.

She abandoned the purpose of her journey and stumbled towards where she perceived the track lay, kicking over the fruits of her previous day's labour in doing so. I knew I must act quickly. I took out my flute and began to play. It was the gentlest of tunes – a lullaby for the troubled, and she responded to my music. I led her gently and invisibly by the hand in case she should stumble in the dark, all the while playing my tune – a soothing, melodic enchantment.

In this way we made progress, retreating further from the village, until I sighted a circular, stone animal shelter in a nearby field. She appeared calm now and followed my music towards its opening. I noticed that she shivered a little in the cold and so I made for her a blanket of hay and soothed her mind until she lay still and content beneath it.

It was best that she slept; best for us both. I myself would sleep no longer though for I needed to consider how I would keep her safe.

Though I had no need of goods in this world I realized that Eva would require provisions. I placed a delicate kiss upon the lids of her sleeping eyes – the lightest of touches, so as not to awaken her and then, safe in the knowledge that she would sleep until dawn, I set off to gather her needs.

By the time she awoke a small fire blazed near the entrance to the shelter. In the meagre light of dawn its warm glow reflected on her face, the early morning breeze causing its flames to dance. From the nearby stream I collected cool, fresh water in an abandoned vessel. Upon the fire I roasted a pigeon and placed by its side ripe peaches from the trees, their skin stretched to bursting by the juicy flesh hidden inside.

I gazed at her in awe as she stretched and stood up, shaking off her body-warmed blanket of hay as she did so. She appeared to be at peace, for which I was grateful. She joined me in front of the fire as an invisible guest and ate the meal I had provided. She sighed with satisfaction and we sat together, enjoying the morning sun once again staking its claim on the earth. The air of calm and the ease with which she satiated her thirst and hunger assured me that - at least for the present - she remained held within the spell of my tune.

I was her guardian – her lord protector, though she did not know it. Yet at the same time I was her jailor. I dared not ask myself if this is what she would have chosen. I dared not judge whether my actions were purely munificent. I dared not consider that if she were to be informed here and now of the extent of atrocity her family and neighbours were suffering, she might rather have chosen to die with them. No – I arrogantly believed that what I was doing was right.

Many years would pass, Dear Reader, before I would come to realize that none of us have the right to deny the choices of an individual, no matter how benevolent our actions seem at the time. All I knew, was that I was bewitched. I had fallen under her spell as readily as she had mine.

*

Death knows no mercy! Misery no bounds! Though Eva and I had travelled many miles from the village I could still hear the cries of the sick, the weeping of mothers, and above all the whoop of joy of his blasphemous laughter. Eva remained deaf to it all. I led her onward, further and further from her home – always gently, never allowing her to tire.

By day we travelled as contented companions through the Gresigne forest, following the path of the Aveyron along the great gorge. By night I ensured her safe rest and protected her from wild animals as a shepherd would his flock.

I thought I had triumphed! I believed without doubt that I was leading her to safety. But where could she be out of harm's way? I should have known that his game would not end at her village. I should have guessed that once he had gorged himself on the population of Penne, still he would not be content. I should have speculated that he too would follow the river, for I had spent long enough now to have learnt that in this world, the way of the water leads to the people.

*

Six days and six nights passed before he came upon us. I smelt the rancid odour of his stinking breath long before I sighted him. As we journeyed an asp viper, black as night, suddenly blocked our path. Swift as a hare I urged her onward, away from the river and into the heart of the forest. But it was pointless – he could travel far more deftly and stealthily than she. There was no way to hide from him. If he was intent on finding someone, he simply would.

He drew along side her, his footsteps falling in with the rhythm of hers. He seemed highly amused at keeping her company without her knowledge. She continued her whimsical journey without query as to why she now walked the undulating ground of the forest floor rather than the level track. The forest grew denser and so darker, the high canopy of the trees eliminating the bright sun. Her long tresses snagged on the branches and her face became wrapped in fine cobwebs, yet she made no attempt to wipe them away, such was she entranced. I was grateful for her composure but my heavy heart beat rapidly with dread at what he might do to her.

I knew that I could lead her on in this way indefinitely but that the journey would be futile. He was playing with her as a cat would a mouse, and I could no longer protect her. His decision would be of his own choosing.

I prompted her to stop. We sat in silence on the damp, mossy ground between two great oaks. I held her cold hand tightly in mine and hoped; hoped that he too would be charmed by her innocence and allow her to live. He continued to study her as we sat, a pondering look upon his pernicious face.

Suddenly he spoke. 'Do you think I cannot see you?'

I assumed it was to Eva that he made the address, but on raising my eyes it was in my direction that he gazed, a cynical smirk upon his face. I believed that my eyes deceived me! I had travelled half way round this world in his company and not once had he acknowledged my existence till now!

He gave a small jeer, his voice deep and strident. 'Indeed I have known you were there since we first arrived in that godforsaken desert! Do you think I did not see your footprints in the sand? Do you think I did not smell your fear or hear your pleading whimpers?' He chuckled, rubbing his filthy hands together in glee at the look of utter shock upon my face. His malodorous breath wafted as he did so, causing my innards to twist. 'I was toying with you! Your despair at my actions entertained me so! Indeed, it was for you that I slaughtered many – just to see you grovel and beg me to stop was so satisfying! I often wondered why you remained in my company. Tell me... Why was it so? Did you secretly thrill at their pain?'

His obscene suggestion reviled me to the core yet I was not brave enough to tell him that I followed him in the hope of destroying him. 'Spare her, I beg of you! Just this one life. She is but an innocent child! She means nothing to you!'

Eva remained silent and merely continued to stare ahead, her eyes fixed on some invisible point in the distance. Despite the tangles in her hair and the dirt which smeared her face she appeared more beautiful than ever.

He sniggered, mocking me. 'Oh, the fool is in love! Shall I end his longing? You cannot have this girl; she is not of your world fool!'

I bit my lip in anger. 'I understand that she cannot be mine but I implore you to spare her life.'

With a soiled finger he prodded the oozing sore at the corner of his mouth and appeared to consider my request. 'I tell you what! We'll strike a deal.' He grinned malevolently. 'Accompany me on the rest of my journey and I will spare her. I have yet to conquer the northern countries of this world – indeed, I have a little something extra up my sleeve for its inhabitants this coming winter!'

*

Dear Reader, I cannot begin to express to you the

enormity of my loathing for him then. Such hatred I have never felt before nor since. I knew though that I had to choose between setting myself free or saving Eva; that was of course if he could be trusted to keep his pledge. But it was my last hope. I had come thus far and was duty bound to go all the way.

My eyes were steely as I gave him my answer. His own continued to mock. 'I shall go with you if you promise to be true to your word.'

Grinning triumphantly, he slapped his thigh. 'You know, you are braver than I credited! Either that, or you are so sick with love for the wench that you would consider her suffering before your own; truly a covert knight in armour!'

He turned then to Eva, his vile hand brushing her hair and stroking the dip of her delicate throat. 'Oh fortunate colleen! Your ghostly champion doth choose your life above his own!'

She remained mute and unseeing and for this I was grateful. The enormity of my revulsion for him was a leviathan!

We sealed our pact. I lifted Eva from the forest floor and carried her home. She slept in my arms for the duration of the journey, her warm scent lingering in my senses long after she had gone. He followed just a pace behind us, though I did not speak again to him.

At the crossroads to her village I placed her gently to her feet and unloosed my charm. As I watched her disappear into the distance the church bell tolled for the dead. My gaze did not leave her until she was a mere memory. I dared not dwell on the horrors she would discover on her return.

Dear Reader, I will spare you the detail of the subsequent years. I'm sure that those of you who are knowledgeable about those times will understand all too well that the great sickness that spread to the northern countries of your world was one of the most abhorrent in history. Suffice it to say that the *something extra* he had in store, was even more vile than the disease he had spread thus far. Your historians have since named it the *pneumonic plague* and for many centuries believed it to spread by rats and fleas.

Only I knew the real perpetrator.

I am informed however that in recent years your experts changed their minds and now believe the disease was airborne. I can only say that they are *getting warmer*.

*

You are probably wondering what became of us both? Well, I shall tell you...

It was several years later that he suddenly declared that he found his work tedious and was off to take some rest. With that he slapped me on the back and declared me free.

As he took his leave of me he uttered a warning; that he was not finished with this world and that he would return when he had something new to offer.

As for me, I believe that I was in a state of shock. By then I was numb to his deeds. I am sad to say that I no longer empathised with the pain or suffering of his victims. I had grown so used to it that my senses were dulled.

I journeyed south for several months until I reached the Sahara Desert, where I bided my time in the company of the Berbers until a passing sandstorm offered a ride home.

So Dear Reader, let my tale be a warning to you all! When you see a door open which you did not expect, do not be afraid of passing through – just be careful as to whom else chooses to step beyond its threshold at your side.

Billabong

In the beginning there was nothing,
Then the serpent emerged from the dark.
It was angry at being awoken,
So it slithered and hissed,
A trail in the void.

It sought out land in which to dwell,
To stake its claim within the realm.
So it called to the spirits,
And earth appeared.
But the earth was cold.

So it called to the spirits,
To thaw the land.
And the sun rose in the sky,
For the very first time,
And warmed the earth.

But the earth grew thirsty,
So it called to the spirits,
To quench its thirst.
And raindrops fell,
And gathered in a pool.

But the pool grew lonely,
Just lying and waiting.
So it called back the serpent,
To reign in its depths,
And it promised it power.

So the serpent returned,
To dwell in the water,
And protect its home,
From all who came later,
And the hole was sacred.

Botany Bay 1790

The speck on the horizon grew larger and larger until it took on a shape. And the shape was winged with billowing, white sails which waved in the breeze. As Bardo squinted into the fierce, mid-day sun the shape drew closer and closer.

As still as a baobab he stood on the shore, watching...

*

Soon ghosts appeared in the body of the vessel and stared towards where Bardo stood. Three hundred white faces, like the sun-bleached corpses of the ancestors, only these ghosts were not dead. They moved and they pointed and they called and they laughed...

And he was bewitched!

'You boy! Don't stand there gawking! Lend a hand!'

Several ghosts dismounted the vessel and staggered towards him, crates in hands as large as boulders and seemingly just as heavy. Still he remained where he stood; black, naked feet forming prints in the sand to later speak of this invasion.

One of the white men, fully clad in heavy black cloth with a strange white ruffle at the neck, pointed a fat, mottled finger in Bardo's face and yelled at him in a strange tongue.

'So the tongue of ghosts is not as the living,' Bardo concluded.

As he roared the face of the ghost blazed red as fire. It seemed to Bardo that this man's anger had ignited a flame within him which was rapidly consuming his body. The fat, fleshy finger pointed in the direction of the vessel. Then Bardo understood what was being demanded; he was required to help the ghosts retrieve the goods from the patient vessel.

His feet unhinged from their rooted position and he ran towards it, noting for the first time that he was one of many who, like him, were now being cajoled and jostled into unloading the abundant goods onto the hot, white sand.

The ghosts worked less quickly, seemingly exhausted. Gasping and puffing they pulled cloths of white from their garments and dabbed at their fleshy brows. Still trickles of sweat ran down their routed foreheads and stung their pale, downcast eyes.

It soon became apparent that these ghosts originated from two distinct clans; those dressed in black, or black and red, gave the orders and did very little work whilst those more dishevelled and ragged were ordered about and treated in much the same way as Bardo and his people. The dishevelled ghosts wore expressions of miserable resignation but uttered no words of complaint.

*

He had fought with every last breath but now the struggle was over. The rough, metal shackles, clasped tight around Bardo's ankles and wrists, left him in no doubt that further effort was fruitless. He lay face down, motionless in the blistering sand. He wondered why it was that the ghosts behaved so; after all, he had come to their aid but now that the vessel was empty he found himself imprisoned in chains. Such behaviour was abhorrent, it was not the way of his people. In his world, people helped one another when need called and all were equally respected.

From his twisted position Bardo was fiercely jerked to his feet by two of the ghosts. Huge, dark eyes glimpsed streaks of red in the sand yet he felt no pain - only fear.

The ghost wearing the white neck ruffle approached and spoke gruffly in the foreign tongue. The struggle had made Bardo unsteady. His head swam and his knees buckled beneath him. As Bardo knelt, the furious ghost kicked hard into the small of his back. Within seconds he was once again yanked to his feet and, wishing to escape a further beating, focussed as hard as he could on steadying his stance by gazing at a far distant spot on the horizon from whence the vessel had come.

Closing his eyes he called in his native tongue to the spirit of his totem - the sea eagle - to give him strength. Presently his heart beat steadied and slowed. When he opened his eyes again it surprised him to see that many others like him were also chained and in various states of submission to the ghosts. Some were mid-fight whilst others were now resigned to their fate.

Along with a number of other young men, Bardo was herded into a group on the sand. The dishevelled ghosts sat in a separate group and appeared every bit as down-hearted as Bardo.

The white ruffle-necked ghost drew with a stick in the sand, all the while speaking in the strange tongue, whilst Bardo and the others looked on in silence. In this way the black-clothed ghosts instructed Bardo and his people to lead the way east to find fresh water and good land. None of the captives spoke and yet it required only a glimpse into his neighbour's eyes to see the fear within the spirit.

Moments later Bardo found himself once again picked out by the white-ruffled ghost, along with another captive of similar stature to him. Their wrist chains were unhinged and they were roughly poked at with a stick and told to lift the ropes which were tied around the handles of one of the trunks. By observing another ghost's mimicry he understood that they were expected to carry the trunk along the sands in order to demonstrate to the rest of his people what they would be asked to do next.

Seven, small shuffles and both captives were down. It would be impossible to carry out this task whilst bound at the feet.

The ruffled ghost screamed at them both, but despite another beating, the second attempt reinforced that this task would not be possible whilst chained.

Bardo and his fellow captive were shoved back towards where his people sat in stunned silence on the sand. The ghosts gathered together, gesturing and muttering in the strange tongue. Once again the white-ruffled ghost stepped forward, pointing and yelling at another of the captives.

The young boy was scrawny and unlikely to have yet been initiated into manhood. He was yanked to his feet and made to stand before the captive audience. The white-ruffled ghost gestured at them to watch whilst he ordered the ankle shackles to be removed from the boy. Reaching into his black coat he retrieved an object which glinted malevolently in the sunlight. It had a handle from which a long, tubular shape protruded.

Gesturing for the boy to run, the ghost aimed the object at the boy's back. The boy's expression spoke of his terror. For a few seconds he did nothing more than emit a whimper and his feet danced on the spot. Eyes of burnt umber locked pleadingly with those of cold steel. A swipe of the chain to the back of his legs however soon made him move. The boy sprinted a few strides in the direction in which the pink finger pointed, before the fat digit squeezed around the handle of the object.

His youthful body slumped in the sand mid-stride, his back bursting into shreds of smoking flesh, causing the captives to jerk and wail in terror. From a gaping, smouldering hole in the spine, his life-blood poured, coagulating quickly in a pool around him.

The captives now understood what would become of them should they try to escape the ghosts.

Bardo's people were unshackled at the feet in order to carry the hoard and Bardo was placed at the head of the chain gang. He knew he must decipher a pathway in the tracks and lead the ghosts to new land. It did not take him long to understand that although to his eyes the tracks were plain to see, to the ghosts they were invisible. In their eyes, every mile of land appeared virtually the same as the previous... and the next... and the next. Bardo hoped to use this to his advantage.

Half a day later and the billabong of Goorialla, the Rainbow Serpent, was sighted. Here they would rest, for the cargo was unyieldingly heavy and Bardo could see that although they did not complain, his people were exhausted. The ghosts walked alongside them carrying nothing and yet Bardo saw that they too were spent. During the journey the ghosts had consumed water from their flasks yet had offered not a drop to Bardo's people.

The heavy chains, linking the captives at the waist, were unlocked and they were allowed to put down their cargo and drink. The ghosts produced food from the crates and ate greedily. Dried biscuits were thrown to the captives but did little to satiate their hunger.

Bardo sat a distance from his companions deep in thought. At this time of year his own clan lived in the opposite direction from whence Bardo had led the ghosts. He had brought them this way in the hope that his own people might remain undisturbed. He now feared he may never see them again.

It was not long before the white-ruffled ghost approached him, encroaching on his melancholy. This time he did not draw in the sand. Instead, from inside his black garment, he produced a rectangular object which appeared to contain several flat, thin layers of yellowed material. With a stick-like object, the ghost created pictures. These drawings depicted a group of dwellings, around which a series of lines appeared to hem them in from the rest of the surrounding land. In a nearby enclosure he drew animals.

Bardo peered closely, beginning to realize what it was that the ghosts wanted. The white-ruffled ghost called to one of his cohort to unlock another of the crates from which he produced a length of rolled up fabric. Upon its unveiling Bardo saw that it bore an angular pattern of red, white and blue. It was swiftly tied to a nearby tree from where it proceeded to wave arrogantly and defiantly in the warm breeze. Though it too was bound, it did not appear to mind.

Then Bardo knew without doubt that the ghosts wished to dwell in these lands, on this very spot, around the sacred billabong of Goorialla. But Bardo knew this must not be. Goorialla could not be disturbed! Whilst it might allow weary travellers to rest and quench their thirst it would never allow these ghostly foreigners to take over the land for themselves. The ancient spirits must not be disturbed in this way. Bardo knew that should they attempt to do so they would pay heavily.

Waving his hand from side to side, he tried to explain this in his native tongue to the white-ruffled ghost but it only served to anger him. Bardo knelt on the ground and with a stick, drew the serpent coiled and at rest in the billabong. He drew the angry face of the serpent swallowing a stick figure of a man and then, in the next drawing, appearing to regurgitate the remains in the form of a rock.

His efforts were to no avail. All it got him was another beating until he bled. When the beating was over and the ghosts once again gathered together, Bardo slowly hauled his beaten body towards where the rest of his people sat watching.

'They want to set up camp here,' he explained. 'I believe they intend to stay in this sacred place for a long time and even keep animals captive here.'

One of the others spoke. 'But we must not be part of it! This land is the ancestral home of Goorialla. The spirit must not be disturbed or it will bring great suffering to those who do so!'

'I agree,' Bardo replied, 'but my attempts at explaining

53

this caused me these wounds.' He gestured to his ribs which were already purpling beneath the leathered skin.

'Then what are we to do?' asked another.

'For now I fear we have no choice other than to do what is requested of us. In the meantime we shall implore the ancestral spirits for compassion and hope that they will see this is not of our doing.'

*

Over the coming days and weeks Bardo and the others were required to collect materials from the land with which to build dwellings for the ghosts. They quickly learned, that if they worked hard and without question or complaint, they were in turn treated reasonably and were at least spared a beating and so, almost without exception, they did so.

Before very long a large village was established and enclosed by a fence. One large hut was erected for Bardo and his men to sleep in. This structure was alien to Bardo's people who preferred to sleep under the stars, but they were no longer permitted to do so. Several other smaller huts were built to house the disorderly men, women and children, and yet another for the ghost leaders. At night Bardo's people were closely guarded so that they could not attempt escape.

During the day they were sent to hunt for food, accompanied by a few of the ghost leaders who appeared to have no hunting skills whatsoever. Were it not for the muskets and other weapons they had brought with them, Bardo knew that survival in this land would be impossible. When he and his men brought back kangaroo meat and cooked it on the open fire they were reviled, preferring to eat from their stash of salted fish. However, over the days, they soon began to realize that if they wanted to survive they could not afford to be so choosy.

When a little free time was granted, Bardo and his men

would gather together to beseech the spirits, especially the spirit of Goorialla, to spare them the travesty they were committing by disturbing this peaceful and sacred place.

It appeared for a while that they might indeed be spared; Goorialla even sent the rains a few times. But this relative peace was not to last...

At dawn, on the thirty-first morning of their arrival, Bardo was jolted from his sleep by a kick to his side.

'Get up!' yelled the white-ruffled ghost whom Bardo now understood to be the chief. 'Where is Williams? What have you done with him you stinking native?'

The angry voice and commotion roused the captives and all now sat alert, regarding the ghost in their midst. The chief ghost pointed his musket from one to the other and repeated his question for all to hear.

The guard assured the chief that none of the captives had left the sleeping hut all night. But of course the question could not be answered. None of the captives had any knowledge as to the whereabouts of the ghost known as Williams. He had simply vanished!

Within the compound there rose much murmuring and muttering until it was established by those who shared Williams' hut that he had left the dwelling shortly before dawn, presumably to relieve himself outside, and had not returned. One or two witnesses from his hut who had been aroused by his departure had simply fallen back to sleep and so had remained unaware of his failure to return.

A search of the nearby forest was carried out and three of Bardo's men were made to enter the billabong in case Williams had drowned. Nothing was found, neither on land nor in water.

Only Bardo and his men knew what had happened, for a walk around the perimeter of the billabong revealed to them a small pile of stones not previously present. These stones they understood to be the regurgitated remains of

Williams. The ghosts did not study the land as they did; to their pale eyes, the arrival of a new pile of stones beside the water was invisible. But to Bardo there was no doubt; Goorialla had awoken and was angry at being disturbed.

*

Over the coming days and weeks several more ghosts disappeared from the compound, and those who remained grew more and more perturbed. All whom were lost belonged to the clan of leaders. With each disappearance one or other of Bardo's group would soon locate a new pile of stones within the compound and then alert the others as to its whereabouts.

As for those left amongst the leading clan however, the disappearance of their men led to disputes and angry discussions. Bardo could tell that the blame lay firmly at the door of one of two clans – his own people and the dishevelled ghost clan. Bardo was an observer; he already understood that the dishevelled clan carried no respect amongst the leading clan. Indeed Bardo had often witnessed them beaten and called names such as *brigand*, *thief* and *murderer,* though what these words meant he had no idea. Yet it was clear by the way in which they were spoken that the terms were derogatory.

With fear came panic and desperation and though they dared not speak of their suspicions, as the number of disappearances increased, some amongst the leading clan began to question in their own minds as to whether there might indeed be supernatural forces at play. Both Bardo's men and the dishevelled captives were watched more closely and rarely were the chief ghosts seen alone.

One night, after a particularly hard day's hunting, Bardo was awoken by a hushed voice. He opened his black eyes and peered into the darkness before him. The white ruffle swam in his vision and for a moment he thought it a dream. Soon a stout finger moved silently in front of him, beckoning to him to follow.

Bardo trailed the chief ghost to a deserted place a little way into the trees. As he had done previously, the chief ghost produced the objects for drawing from his clothing. This time he attempted to replicate the serpent swallowing a man which Bardo had previously drawn for him. All the time he spoke to Bardo beseechingly. A few words were by now understood between the ghosts and the captives but most communication was still by means of facial expression and gesture. By using these clues Bardo understood that he was being asked if he thought it possible that the disappearances of the ghosts had been caused by the Serpent Spirit.

Bardo had feared the white-ruffled ghost since the very first day. He had not forgotten the callous way in which he had murdered the young boy on the sand nor the beatings he had himself received from him. For a moment he was hesitant about sharing his own beliefs with such a being. Raising his eyes from the drawings he summoned the courage to meet the eyes of the ghost. The expression was one of fear – pure, unadulterated fear but also something else – desperation. Bardo knew that this chief, this man of high esteem, would not have come to him like this unless desperate.

The stick and pad were thrust into Bardo's own hands. Never having handled such tools before Bardo found them difficult to master at first, but was crudely able to confirm what the ghost himself now considered possible – that the spirit of Goorialla had indeed been rudely disturbed by the building of the compound and was now set on revenge.

'What can be done?' the chief ghost pleaded, and Bardo smelt his fear and felt pity. 'If you can find a way to put an end to this I promise that you and your people will be granted your freedom soon. We needed your help in finding and building a place to live and to teach us to hunt but now we are beginning to master these skills for ourselves.'

Though Bardo could not understand the words being spoken he was aware of a sincerity not previously witnessed. He pondered his options for a moment before communicating that a shaman should be sent for to advise them about what, if anything, they could do to appease the spirits. It was agreed that on the following day Bardo would be accompanied on his journey back home to bring back the shaman.

Back in his sleeping place he worried about unveiling the ancestral home to his captors and so, in his mind, weaved a pathway through the tracks which would lead the way home in such a way that it would not be remembered by the ghost. He knew that before long his people would be moving on to the next place, for the hunting season was soon to change.

*

As they approached the camp Bardo implored the guard to remain hidden in the bush whilst he himself entered. The guard was reluctant, fearing that Bardo might run away, but when Bardo gestured that the guard may be overcome he grudgingly agreed on condition that Bardo remain in sight.

Musket cocked, the guard watched closely as Bardo was greeted warmly by his people. He could see that they had missed him and were anxious to know where he had been. After talking to an elderly member of the tribe, who was heavily daubed in a variety of coloured pigments, Bardo gestured for the guard to enter. Now it was his turn to feel as Bardo had once done. His knees trembled. Sweat ran down his chest and pooled at the waistband. He approached slowly, all the while regarded by a hundred curious eyes.

The elderly, painted man stepped forward, a look of disquiet upon his weather worn face. He gesticulated and spoke in a tongue that meant nothing to the guard. Bardo explained that the man was *Maban;* he could see what others could not. Bardo drew in the sandy ground. The drawing, though crude, was identifiable as that of the Maban, only Bardo drew him with three eyes. He was to accompany them back to the village to see if anything could be done.

*

Just as the three men re-entered the village the sun set low on the horizon. The air was still and warm and the sky had been paint-washed golden pink. Work had stopped for the day and all three clans were disparately seated in various parts of the compound. As the Maban approached, murmurs echoed around the camp. The ruffled ghost stepped forward, keen to establish himself as chief, but for the first time he smiled at Bardo.

The Maban called for silence and all were hushed. He approached the billabong and knelt before it. Chanting in a tongue that only Bardo and his men understood he entreated the spirits to reveal themselves. Bardo's eyes skimmed the crowd of white ghosts, expecting them to mock, and was surprised when no-one did. The chanting and dancing of the Maban captivated all; even the unkempt ghost-children were silent. With hollow eyes and shaven heads they watched, scratching at sores atop their heads.

As the Maban turned to face the crowd the spell was broken. For at that very second a bolt of lightning shot from the sky and struck the ground just beyond the enclosure. The crowd gasped; the sky had previously born no sign of a storm.

'Namarrgon the Lightning Spirit is watching.' Bardo

heard the words echo amongst his people.

The white-ruffled ghost and Bardo were summoned to sit with the Maban a little way off.

'You must leave this place,' demanded the Maban. 'The spirits of our ancestors are angry. Goorialla has been greatly disturbed. It has taken revenge by feeding on your men but it will not be satisfied until its sacred home is returned. I have asked the spirits to grant you time so that you may gather your belongings and take down what you have built. This land must be returned to peace or you will all be destroyed!'

It was just as Bardo had feared since the day of arrival. He wondered how he might be able to persuade the chief ghost that moving on and re-building elsewhere was the only option. He knew, that even if the chief believed this place could never offer them what they sought, the other ghosts would not be so easily persuaded.

The chief ghost sat on the ground in stunned silence. By now the sun had set. Night-crickets mocked a rhythmic tune. Bardo could hear the people of the compound returning to their huts, preparing to await the news.

The Maban now turned to Bardo. 'We must gather our people and tell them to make music and sing to the spirits so that they may be distracted for a while. This will give these people chance to pack up and leave.'

Bardo knew that the Maban was right. He returned to his people and gathered them close. They encircled the billabong and took up the dance. From the huts of the ghost clans they came... and they watched... and they listened. Charmed by what they saw and heard, most understood what needed to be done.

At sunrise next morning, all were jolted from their slumber by the sound of a piercing cry. Bardo leapt from his sleeping pad and hurried outside. Already a crowd was gathered around the billabong. His sleep-disturbed eyes scanned the mob. Where were the ghost leaders? No black or red costumes were anywhere to be seen.

Joined by others from his hut he headed towards the billabong, pushing his way to the front of the crowd. There, in the midst of the water, protruded a large, smooth rock, shaped like a mound. On its summit lay a sleeping serpent. Oblivious to the raised voices around it, it slept on peacefully in the early morning sun, the reflection of its rainbow-patterned skin rippling in the clear water.

Then a voice rose up from the crowd. 'We are free! The guards are gone! This land is ours to do with as we wish!' Nods of assent were witnessed amongst the bedraggled ghost-clan and cheers of agreement spread swiftly around the billabong.

Bardo raised his arm and shouted for them to listen. Lost in their celebration they did not want to hear. Within minutes the guards' huts were rampaged and barrels of rum brought and shared amongst all. There was much whooping and calling, dancing and shouting. All was madness!

Bardo retreated to his hut and soon returned carrying the gumleaf which he had crafted. Standing before the crowd he blew a long, high note. The crowd fell silent. 'You are not free! You cannot stay here! The spirits have punished the guards for encroaching on this land, but if you stay here the same will happen to you! I will lead you to new land. It will only take a few days to reach. You can begin again. I beseech you – do not be foolish!'

But the ghosts would not listen; they refused to hear. Even after all they had witnessed their memory was short-lived. They would pay no heed to Bardo's warning.

So Bardo gathered his own people and they left the compound once more as free men.

The days passed and the season to move on arrived.

Bardo's clan followed the ancient tracks through the forests until they drew close to the place where the compound had stood. Whilst his people rested in the shade Bardo continued along the track to the billabong. The approaching silence filled his ears. Bardo knew that he would discover no life there. It was almost as if the compound had never existed. If it were not for the fence Bardo might think he had dreamt it.

He stood at its outer limits and peered beyond. To the eyes of the ghosts it would have appeared as nothing more than a pond in the middle of a barren field.

But Bardo saw plenty. He saw the discolouration of the earth where the huts had once stood. He saw that the billabong no longer held a large rock in its belly, and he saw that its surrounding land was stonier than that outside its perimeter.

With trembling fingers he reached beyond the fence and picked up one of the stones. It was warm to the touch. He turned it over to reveal its rougher underbelly. Squinting closely, he picked off a tiny fragment of white fabric. Hurling the stone beyond the fence and into the dark realm of the billabong he returned to his people.

Mine

'Back to work girl, else I'll dock your pay!' Anna's heart leapt as the master's gruff voice woke her. Two round eyes, encircled by coal dust, sprung open and attempted to locate the whereabouts of her castigator – an impossibility in the liquorice-black.

As a trapper her job was to open and close the air-doors to allow the carts to pass through. It was bitterly cold, dank and the hours passed by as slow as Father Time. Yet she did not fear the dark. Even when her gas lamp died and she was thrown into its totality she was not afraid, for she had worked in this mine for just over a year – since the day following her eleventh birthday to be precise and had grown used to it.

Not even the rats caused her to scare any longer, for they never attacked; they simply went about their own business, as did everyone else, until it was time to surface again into daylight. Except at this time of year it was no longer daylight when they finally surfaced. It was mid-December and fast approaching the shortest day. Night when she left home, and night again when she returned; at least that was what the sky would have her believe.

But today she was afraid; in fact she had hardly caught a wink the previous night. It was the worry that did it – fretting about what she had discovered and what it might mean for her future, for all their futures. It was this lack of sleep rather than the tedium of the work which had caused her eyelids to droop heavily and to burn, until she could no longer keep them open, and so had given in to their persistent weight.

Once the loaded cart had rumbled by on its journey, she sat and thought. She was no longer tired now, for the master's voice had startled her into full wakefulness. Her empty, gnawing stomach churned nervously as she considered what to do next.

*

It had been a month since the master had escorted her to the office at the end of her shift. 'A quiet word,' he'd said, tapping the side of his nose with his forefinger as he'd led the way. Anna had fretted, and yet his manner had not seemed reproachful, in fact his demeanour had seemed slightly more pleasant than usual – even if somewhat insincere.

On entering the unfamiliar office she had been surprised to see the mine owner, Mr Peningrade, leaning back in his chair on the other side of a large, wooden desk, his expensive leather boots - the type only worn by the gentry - defying good manners by resting on the desk. He had stared at her with piercing eyes of steely blue, and without thinking she had bowed her head and dropped a small curtsy.

'Your name is Anna I believe?' he had begun amicably enough. 'You have been here a year already? Are you enjoying your work?'

Anna considered this a rather strange question. One did not enjoy ones work here; one simply tolerated it as a means of helping the family afford the basic necessities. However, she had smiled and nodded, still without raising her eyes. 'Yes Sir. Of course Sir.'

He had waved his hand then, flippantly, in the direction of Mr Harris, known to one and all as *The Master* before continuing. 'Harris has been telling me that you are a hard worker and that you never scare or slack in your duties, nor do you complain or whine as do most others your age.' She sensed his eyes boring into her even though she continued to stare at her feet.

66

'Thank you Sir.'

'Well Anna,' he paused for a second. 'Harris and I have been wondering... Would you like a change?'

'How do you mean Sir?'

'Are you trustworthy Anna?'

'Of course Sir!' She flexed her toes inside her heavy, black boots, though whether out of nervousness or because they were already a year old she was not entirely sure. She only knew that something felt – wrong. She felt awkward, embarrassed. Her feet were eager to by their leave.

He leaned towards her, whiskey-tainted breath caressing her face as he spoke. 'How would it be if I were to offer you higher wages, let's say one and a half times what you are paid now, for doing the exact same job?'

At last she raised her eyes and looked at him. The corners of his mouth were curled in a smile, only it was more of a smirk, for his eyes did not reciprocate.

'How do you mean Sir?'

His voice became a whisper. 'Can you keep a secret Anna?' he continued, watching her intently, the number eleven furrowing his dark brows.

He is rather handsome, Anna thought. Yet there is something not quite right about him. She searched his face as he awaited her reply...

'Well girl?' The question, delivered with a little impatience, caused her to jump.

'Yes Sir. That is as long as the secret will bring me or my family no harm Sir.'

He clicked his tongue against the roof of his mouth. 'Of course it will bring you no harm girl! Only if you agree to the job you cannot tell anyone else about it. Do you understand? Not even your mother.'

'But I thought you said the job would be the exact same, only better paid?'

His expression grew pensive. 'And so it is. It's just in

a different part of the mine, a new shaft, that's the only difference.'

She was confused; she could not begin to think why this would need to be kept secret, nor could she comprehend his offer of higher wages, but she was too afraid to articulate her thoughts. He continued to watch her closely. She shifted her weight awkwardly in the clumsy boots.

Without her noticing, The Master had crept round to her side of the desk. He too now scrutinised her countenance, a lopsided grin on his gin-whiskered face.

'But Sir, if you don't mind me saying, my mother will know that I have a different job when I take home more wages.'

'And that must be part of the secret Anna. The extra money is for you alone, to do with as you wish.' He saw her hesitate. He knew only too well that such children were as loyal to their parents as was a knight to his King. 'Of course, if you do not wish to spend the money on yourself then you can squirrel it away, and should your family ever face hard times, then it might come in useful. Might it not?' He witnessed a pinch of guilt line her face, only to be swiftly replaced with joy. He knew she was imagining how it would feel to help the family out of a bad situation. Temptation was beginning to win her round.

'I suppose so,' she muttered, though if truth be told she could not imagine being able to resist handing the extra wages over to her mother. Surely she could just let her into the secret? Any thought of that however was soon quashed.

'I mean it though Anna! No-one. Absolutely no-one can be told, you understand?'

She felt a little afraid; she did not want to turn down this opportunity but had never before been disloyal to her parents. Perhaps she should agree, then wait and see what the secret was. That way she could truly make up her mind. She nodded towards him and managed a small smile.

'Then you shall begin on Monday,' he said, returning the gesture. 'Now let me explain a little more. Not a word mind, don't forget.'

And so he had explained that she was to work in a deeper part of the mine, a part where only a few, select workers toiled, and that this particular shaft had been recently struck. He had assured her that it posed no danger, and that they'd simply recently discovered a *special* kind of coal there – one which would reward them with greater profit. The reason for the secret, he had explained, was that this special coal could only be found in this particular part of the mine and it would therefore be unwise to share its location with *all and sundry*, in case the *avaricious powers that be*, should wish to expand.

He did not want to be greedy, he had said. He merely wanted to take advantage of this superior fossil whilst it was available. Apparently this particular fossil required specialist extraction which was why only a handful of more competent miners would be employed there. After all he *did not want any Tom, Dick or Harry thinking they could have a whack at it and causing a fall*.

Whilst Peningrade had explained all of this to her The Master's eyes had not once left her face. He was judging her, she knew. She flushed, and hoped he did not notice her discomfort.

All this had happened just over a month ago, and since then she had turned up for work as usual. But instead of entering shaft one cage with the rest of the miners, she was escorted a little further along the pit surface and in through a shed-like building where, along with four other miners, she would enter shaft two.

None of the four ever spoke to her, nor did she recognize any of them as being from the village. This she considered rather strange, as miners were almost without exception locally sourced. Everything else was the same though. She would exit the cage when it reached pit bottom and walk the few hundred yards, half bent, to her door, where she would spend the rest of the day exactly as she had done before – waiting for the familiar tug on the rope and the bell which would summon her to open it. The only other difference was that at the end of the first week, and the consecutive three weeks, instead of receiving her shilling wages she would collect a shilling and sixpence.

She didn't really know how she had managed to keep it secret from her mother. It was just that somehow she felt it would be more disloyal to talk about her new job than it would to hide the extra wages. And so it was not without a substantial amount of guilt that she had so far stashed away the extra two shillings in an old tobacco tin, high up in the toilet cistern at the bottom of their yard. Yes, this constituted a risk, but at least when visiting the privy she had the space to herself, whereas there was nowhere else in the little two up, two down cottage which she shared with her parents, two brothers and sister which granted such privacy.

Then it had all changed...

At first the only thing which she had noticed as different in this part of the mine was that when the coal carts passed by, their contents were covered in tarpaulin, as if the miners did not wish anyone to see inside. She dismissed this though, as the owner had already explained to her that this particular seam of coal was special.

It wasn't until the fourth week that it suddenly dawned on her that something else was amiss. It was the sound that the carts made as they journeyed back and fore. She wondered why it had taken her a whole month to notice, but now that she had she could not get it out of her mind.

In the previous mine she had become as familiar with the rumble of the carts as the sound of her own breathing; after all, there was little else to entertain the mind during a day's work underground. The eyes had little on which to focus; the nose knew only a musty dankness and so, after a while, one's sense of hearing became heightened.

The fifth cart of the morning had rumbled by on its journey to pit top when she suddenly realized that it sounded hollow. She waited for its return some fifteen minutes later and listened carefully...

She was not mistaken! This time the rumble was deeper, as if the cart were now full. Strange, she thought. Why would the cart sound empty on the way out of the mine and full on the way in? It had puzzled her for the remainder of the day and she had subsequently found herself tuned in to each cart that passed by.

Thinking about it, it was also strange that the miners with whom she made the daily journey underground, and intermittently saw during the day, never made any effort to speak to her; in fact, they almost behaved as if she were not there.

In the previous mine shaft she had found almost all the miners rather jovial. There existed a spirit of comradeship underground – each worker keenly aware of the potential dangers of the job and thus always on the lookout for the other. They had always chatted to her and had often offered words of kindness as they passed by her door with their laden carts.

At first she had assumed that the silence of these miners was due to the fact that the owner had employed them from another town – perhaps a place where he owned another mine. She supposed that as she was a stranger to them, they did not speak to her out of shyness. However, four weeks on she now found their silence disconcerting – unfriendly almost. In fact, when she thought about it, they did not speak to each other either. It had become quite uncomfortable – the way in which they all made the short journey to pit bottom together, plunged into total darkness, and yet it was as if each undertook the journey alone.

She sat puzzled. Often her mother scolded her for allowing her imagination to run away with her; in fact, she had on several occasions warned Anna that what she termed an over-active mind would one day land her in trouble. The problem was though, that the day passed by so slowly underground that one had little else to do other than use one's imagination.

She often wished she could go to school and had taken to arithmetic, reading and writing quite readily at Sunday School. But unfortunately the financial situation of her family, like all the other families in their village, was unable to support such a luxury as regular schooling.

Her thoughts returned to her problem. What could she possibly do about this conundrum? Her ears were telling her that the coal carts were entering the mine full and leaving empty. But how could that be? If only she could somehow take a peek inside one of the carts as they passed, then she would know for certain!

She watched more closely to see if there was a way in which she could see under the tarpaulin but there was not. In fact the tarpaulin was tied in place with sturdy-looking rope.

It wasn't until after several days of pondering this puzzle that she came up with a solution. She knew that about four hours into the day, (one became fairly accurate at time-counting despite the absence of a clock) the miners took a short lunch break. It was not that she actually witnessed this, but for approximately thirty minutes or so, no carts came or went. She had taken to eating her own meagre lunch at the same time, always alone and in the bleak darkness, with only the constant drip of water for company. Still, slowly chewing on her crust of bread broke the monotony for a short while.

She knew that not far along from where they entered the shaft at pit bottom there was a small cut-away where stood a tatty, wooden bench and a few spare tools. Perhaps this was where the miners took their break.

At the start of shift on the fourth day she looked more closely, counting the number of paces from the assumed lunch spot to the place where the coal carts came to rest at the end of the track. It was a distance of eleven paces. If she was correct and they did indeed eat at this spot, perhaps she could wait for them to break for lunch then follow the cart and peer inside.

Anna knew this would be risky as sound was amplified within the hollow shaft of the mine. She could only hope that they would at least make conversation with each other during lunch break - once she was out of earshot - and that such conversation might allow her to creep up to the cart undetected. If her plan failed and they saw her she would have no choice other than to feign illness, as once one's shift as a trapper began one did not have permission to leave one's spot until the end of the shift – not even to visit the privy.

And so her plan was hatched for the following day...

The morning had passed by in its usual monotonous way except for the fact that Anna's stomach had lurched every time she thought about what she planned to do. Over the past few days, ever since she had begun to suspect them, she had attempted to get a better look at the miners during their journey to pit bottom. However, their clothing, along with the helmets, left little to see. Besides, she could do little more than take a cursory glance at their expressions before being plummeted into the darkness of the journey. They were a serious bunch though – emotionless almost. Of that she had no doubt.

Over the past four days she had counted the number of cart journeys made during the morning shift and had found it consistently to be eight. Therefore, as expected, after the passing of the eighth cart, the four miners passed by her door and disappeared out of sight further along the track. She waited, fully alert, heart racing...

Silence.

After just a few moments she removed her heavy pit boots and proceeded to creep along the dark, wet track in the same direction as the cart. Remaining silent was difficult. She believed that even her heartbeat echoed around the sodden, dank walls of the mine, and would surely give her away. Once or twice her bare, frozen feet slipped on the wet floor, causing her to stumble. It was all she could do not to cry out.

Eventually, after what seemed an age, she saw it – the last cart to have passed her by now stood patiently waiting at the end of the track. The four miners sat, as she had anticipated, within the cut-away a little further along. Now, if her theory was correct, this cart, instead of being laden with the black gold, would be empty. She paused to listen, hoping that their conversation would conceal her footsteps as she approached the cart.

At first she was disappointed to discover that although she could hear faint sounds as they shifted about still they did not talk. She decided that she could not afford to have come this far only to back down and so, stealthy as a fox, she continued to advance inch by inch towards the cart.

She was within touching distance! Retrieving the small

knife which she had slipped into the pocket of her tunic before leaving home, she edged closer and closer...

Just as she reached the corner of the tarpaulin she heard a voice. She stopped, still as the dead, and listened. One of the men had spoken. She strained her hearing, trying to decipher what he said, but could not understand a word. She stood still, breathing shallowly, convinced that they would hear her. As another answered, she knew she was not mistaken. They were speaking a language foreign to her ears. Never before had she heard such words nor such an accent. Now she understood why it was that they never spoke to her! Peningrade had not only employed them from out of the village but from another country altogether!

But why? She could not begin to think of any logical reason for this. Deciding to forget about it for the present, she turned her attention back to the task in hand.

Precariously, she held onto one of the ropes which fastened the tarpaulin, and with the other hand she began to saw at it with the knife. It seemed to take forever. At any moment she expected to hear a shout of discovery. She was grateful that the miners continued to talk to each other, as at least their indecipherable conversation helped to cover the sound of the sawing which, to her ears, seemed to reverberate around the walls.

Finally the rope gave and she managed to haul her small body up on to the cart and slip her freezing fingers, now almost numb with cold, inside. Yes! She had been right about the sound. The cart was indeed empty!

Theory proven, she hastily re-fastened the rope and scurried, quick as a rat, back along the track to her door. She had made it, and in doing so had not only proven herself right but had also discovered that these particular miners were foreign! She slipped her work boots back on her numb feet and slumped against the air-door breathlessly. A mixture of fear and relief washed over her. Empty though her stomach was, she was unable to face her meagre lunch.

What a discovery! But what was it all about? Why did the carts return from the pit surface full and leave empty? The whole purpose of mining was to retrieve what the ground offered up and take it above to be used – not the other way round.

So exhausted was she by the stress of having completed her mission that she could not focus on a possible solution, nor could she think of anyone who might be willing to believe her should she tell them what she had discovered. There was probably some simple and logical reason that would make her look completely foolish, as well as cause her to lose her job, if she confided the secret.

It was not until she was tucked up safely in bed that night that the solution came to her. If she really couldn't live with her discovery then she would simply have to find a way of following the cart in the opposite direction, deeper into the mine.

But how could she do this without being discovered? Yes, she could wait for the strange miners to take their break as previously and then follow the track in the opposite direction, but that would only provide her a maximum of fifteen minutes before she would need to return again in order to open the doors for their return journey. The only other solution was a dangerous one, and one which would involve not only a substantial amount of risk but also a lie!

The previous mine in which she had worked operated both day and night. Most of the miners from the village worked shifts, but she herself had never had to work the night shift and for this she was grateful. She had quickly discovered however that the mine in which she now worked only operated during the daytime.

On returning home the following day the lie was given.

'Mum, I've been asked to work a double shift on Friday. There's some important maintenance that needs to be carried out and The Master's asked if I'll work it – just this once.' Anna could barely look her mother in the eye as she spoke the words and so busied herself pretending to unpick a knotted bootlace.

She sensed her mother's hesitation, even though she had not yet spoken in reply, and so quickly added, 'They've said they'll pay me an extra sixpence if I do it – that'll help won't it? And they've said I can rest up for a few hours in between.' The guilt tore at her, knowing that she could easily retrieve the extra money from its hiding place to help placate her mother's worries. Times were hard and every little extra was a bonus.

'Well I'm not keen Anna, you've never been away from home at night, and besides a double shift will exhaust you.'

'I'll be fine Mum, honest. It's only the once and if I don't like it I'll say no in future if they ask me again.'

'Well if you're sure, but I won't allow this to become a regular thing you know. I hate sending you down there as it is never mind having you down that hole at night! I won't sleep a wink.'

Anna leapt up and planted a kiss on her mother's cheek before she could change her mind. 'Thanks Mum, the extra money'll be handy and I really don't mind.' Anna tried to relax, but what she was to do come Friday churned her insides and stole into her dreams, making her sleep fitful.

When Friday arrived she did not even dare to cast a glimpse at the miners as she accompanied them on the usual short journey underground. The day shift passed by as slowly as the night before Christmas. At five thirty the siren announcing the end of shift was sounded as usual and Anna duly made her way back to the cage.

The fact that the lamp room for this shaft was unmanned

had previously worried her a little, since this had meant there was no-one to collect her lamp token at the beginning of shift and no-one to return it at the end. She knew this meant that no-one therefore checked whether or not all of the miners were safely returned to pit-top.

Over the past few days she had watched closely, as one or other of the alien miners simply pulled the lever to operate the winding gear before making their silent ascent.

Not once had she noticed them doing a head count, nor had any of them ever appeared to look out for her safety. Once the cage jolted to a halt at pit top they would merely exit without a second glance in her direction.

Now she hoped to turn this to her advantage. She hoped and prayed that nothing would go wrong...

As soon as the last man was out of the cage she quickly pulled on the lever. Her heart pumped like a bellows in her chest and a cackle of fluid from her lungs made her cough as she journeyed back down into the blackness.

Lantern ready, she scuttled along the tracks until she reached her air door. Strange how somewhere so bleak could bring one comfort merely through familiarity, she thought. She rested on the ground, her back against the air door, until her breathing steadied, before mustering up the courage to take the next step on her journey...

She was sure she must have walked at least a mile along the track. Her lantern provided her little comfort and she was glad that she had tied a spare to her belt in case this one failed. All would be lost if that should happen.

She could not be certain in the sameness of the mine but she had a feeling that the track she was following, sloped gradually downwards– deeper and deeper underground. Every now and then she paused in her tracks and listened to the nothingness, just to be certain that she was not being followed. Raising her lantern to examine the walls of the mine, she could see that no source material had been extracted here. So far the mine merely consisted of the usual length of dripping, black tunnel. The roof was lower in some parts than others, and was supported by the familiar, wooden beams. Nothing untoward then – except for a total lack of evidence of any mining having taken place which served only to reinforce her theory that these miners, instead of taking coal from here to pit top, were in actual fact reversing the process and taking it back underground along these very tunnels.

But what possible explanation could there be for this strange procedure? She half-wished at this moment that she was more like her brothers and simply prepared to accept without question. However she was not. Once an itch tickled she could not keep her hands off it.

On and on she crept, and the nothingness continued. Now and then small shards of coal freckled the tracks but apart from that there was nothing. The deeper she went, the more determined she became. After all, she had all night! This thought made her smile in the darkness, even though she was still half-afraid of what she would find at the end – if indeed there was an end.

What did she expect to find? She had given this little consideration over the past few weeks. She supposed that in all probability the tunnel would merely come to an abrupt end – a halt which would signal that she could simply go no further. Then why was it that she had been so determined to undertake this adventure? She must be stupid!

Suddenly a wave of fear caused her bowels to twist. What if she discovered nothing then had to return all the way back to the pit-bottom only to learn that she could not operate the cage to return to pit top? That would definitely give her away as she would be able to do nothing other than wait for the miners to return on Monday and find her! And how would she survive without food? Even worse – her mother would alert the authorities if she did not arrive home early Saturday morning and they would surely search for her! What was she doing? She hesitated, about to turn back, but instead sat a while, gulping deep breaths of dank air.

After several minutes of restful calm she continued along the tunnel. In the faint beam of lamplight she was sure she could see a low door in the distance. She crawled towards it, half expecting to find someone waiting for her there. Upon reaching it she saw that it was as simply made as the one which she operated. Tentatively, she pushed...

The door opened to reveal a wider cavernous area, similar in appearance and size to that which began at pit bottom – only here, no cage stood waiting to take her to the top. Instead, on turning in a circle, she discovered to her left yet another door, this one appearing to be made of robust, dark metal. Her eyes, used to the darkness of the mine, detected around its border the merest glimpse of light – a sunset-hued glow. Her heart beat fast. Dare she attempt to open it? She had come this far and yet even now did not know if her courage would fail her.

She paused a while, palms clammy, her face grimy with sweat and coal dust. She saw plainly that the door was fastened from the inside by a sturdy, metal, sliding bolt. Slowly, cautiously, she wiggled it open...

Her eyes fixed on the crack of light; the door opened a fragment at a time. At any moment she expected someone to attack or at least reproach her from the other side. But why would anyone expect her arrival? Her eyes gradually adjusted until they were able to focus on what secrets were about to be revealed...

Disbelief! Confusion and shock! Anna gazed into a moody, thunderous purple sky which, every few seconds, was lit by ferocious flashes of acidic, green lightning...

And at eye level – an environment so alien, it could not possibly be of her world! This was the stuff of nightmares! The land was so barren – so desolate; stripped of any worth, like one would imagine if the world ended. The only identifiable object was an empty, abandoned coal cart, which stood a little way off to the left, its wooden slats rotted and broken, its rusty legs and feet rendering it redundant.

Too afraid to step into this world, she watched from the crack in the door. How could she have failed to notice the noise? Her ears were filled with a mechanical, droning sound, as though the very land groaned beneath a mighty weight and was about to give way. Metal on metal? No-lower pitched – rock against rock. Nothing as far as the eye could see – just rocks of cinnabar and raw umber, so jagged along their surface that it would be impossible to walk along them without tearing open one's feet. Here and there, what appeared to be burnt tree stumps, littered the ravaged ground. And all the while the monotonous, droning filled the air, repetitive and menacing in its tone.

And Anna knew now, without any doubt, that this was not her world.

Enough! She had seen enough! With trembling fingers she re-bolted the door then she scurried back through the length of the mine as quickly as her breath and strength would allow.

She was spent! The nervous anxiety of the past few weeks, along with the physicality of the actual journey, had rendered her exhausted! On reaching the comfort of her door she lay curled on the ground, chest heaving, saliva straining at her throat – too exhausted to acknowledge the thirst and hunger which tore at her body. No. It was her aching mind to which she needed to address first.

Gradually her panting eased and, trembling with fatigue, she made her way towards the cage. Luck was on her side! The switch kicked into motion, slowly but surely, delivering her to safety.

The clock in the cage room announced that it was one o'clock in the morning. Her mind and body ached to rush home to the comfort and safety of her bed, but she knew if she did so, her mother's suspicions would be raised. After all, she had told her she was working the night shift and that would not be over until 5:00a.m.

Finding a relatively clean and dry adult-sized coat she stepped out of her sodden clothing, washed her filthy hands and face in a bucket of cold water, and sat down on a wooden bench to eat.

Never before had she experienced such utter exhaustion! Still – in just a few hours she would be able to go home and rest properly; then she would need to decide what it all meant and what, if anything, she should do about her discovery.

*

Just as she had guessed, her mother had the tin bath ready in front of the fire. Steaming bubbles and a dry towel awaited. Luxury! Once undressed and alone Anna was surprised to find that warm, salty tears trickled down her face, racing to join the pool in which she sat. Frustration, that's what it was! A combination of frustration and sheer exhaustion because she never cried! Swiftly she swept away the tears, in case her mother should return to scrub her back. If she witnessed her crying Anna knew she would feel guilty for allowing her to have worked the night shift.

Over a warm, honey-sweetened bowl of porridge, Anna considered her options...

Again and again the only plausible solution she could come up with was that she could do no more on her own. Who, therefore, did she trust enough to divulge what she had learned? Who would not merely dismiss her theory as the ramblings of a child with an over-active imagination?

There was only one person – Mr Williamson, office manager at the pit and also the teacher at Sunday School. He was one of the kindest and most thoughtful adults she knew, and she hoped that he would at least listen and consider what she had to say without informing her parents or jeopardising her job.

And so on Sunday, after school, when everyone else had gone home, she hung around pretending to tidy away the bibles. She approached him nervously. 'Mr Williamson, I have a problem that is burning away inside me, and... and I can't tell anyone, but I really need to. I think it could be very significant.'

He came to her side, an earnest look upon his face. 'Whatever is the matter Anna?'

Her voice was a nervous sob. 'If I tell you, you must promise not to tell anyone, not even my mother. I could lose my job if anyone finds out and we can't afford for that to happen. I desperately need your help.'

'Sit down Anna.' His brows furrowed above the reading glasses which sat low on the bridge of his nose.

She took a deep breath. 'Where shall I begin?'

Slowly the whole story unravelled. She did not miss out a single detail. From time to time she glanced at him in order to assess his thoughts and was surprised to see no sign of disbelief or amusement.

When she had finished she sighed so heavily that her shoulders dropped several inches. Now she studied his face. For several seconds he remained silent; his brow remained furrowed and she could have sworn that his pallor had paled.

'I'm very glad that you have come to me Anna,' he began in earnest. 'And I can share something with you. I too have had my suspicions about activities over in shaft two for some time. I have always been entirely trusted to run the accounts of the mine and yet, when Peningrade purchased it from the previous owner just under two years ago, I saw that he soon opened a new shaft – the one in which you are now employed, and yet I was never asked to see to any of the accounts or paperwork attached to it.

In addition the miners you talk about – I do not know their names nor have I ever had to make out their wages. It's as if the second shaft is a great secret, with only the handful of miners, Harris and Peningrade having access to it; a classified operation. I have indeed been very curious about it myself.'

Anna exhaled a loud sigh of relief. Just knowing that she was not alone in her suspicions meant so much. 'But what could possibly be going on?' she asked. 'I feel as if I am going crazy even suggesting that the shaft leads to another world.'

Mr Williamson remained deep in thought for a minute or so. 'Describe for me again Anna, this other world that you say the shaft leads to.'

'Well, as I said, I only saw it through a crack in the door but it appears completely pillaged! It's virtually barren except for a few burnt tree stumps here and there; the whole land is practically razed. And the colours are all – well – wrong! The sky is moody and purple with constant flashes of acid-green lightning. It just looks as if it's all – destroyed. I'm afraid I'm not very good at explaining; only I've never seen anything like it. And one of the worst things, the scariest things, is the noise! There's a constant droning sound, only it changes pitch, as if huge forces are rubbing against each other and are about to give way. I don't know. It's hard to explain!'

He sat deep in thought, nervously twisting the corners of his moustache with forefinger and thumb. 'You know Anna, some might call me mad, but from what you describe it sounds as if this other world has been depleted, as if whoever inhabits it has used up their resources and there is nothing left. Maybe this is why they take our coal; perhaps they have no fuel of their own left.' He laughed. 'What am I saying? It sounds mad even to my ears!'

'But it must be! It sounds insane but I know we're right. There can't be any other possible explanation for taking coal there. The thing is what can we do?'

He paused again. 'For the time being Anna, I think the best thing is simply to continue as if nothing has happened. Carry on with your work and do not let them become suspicious of you. In the meantime I'll keep a close eye on them – Harris and Peningrade too. We'll speak again after chapel next Sunday, alright?'

Another week passed by and Anna did her best to appear as though nothing was amiss. The following Sunday, during the lesson in the little chapel, she just knew that Mr Williamson had news for her. Once again she waited until all the others had left before sitting down at the front of the chapel where they would not be overheard should someone come to the door.

'I watched them Anna! I watched them after work every day this week,' he began excitedly. 'I've noticed that Peningrade tends to visit the mine on Monday afternoons which is rather strange for an owner; the last one hardly ever came near the place. At five thirty I switched off the lights in the office as usual and locked it, then crept round to the back of shaft two and hid. I didn't need to wait long. Just half an hour after the shift was over and you'd all gone home they returned, all six of them! Harris, Peningrade and the four miners. They seemed a little jittery and did not speak to one another, but they entered the cage room, and within moments I heard it descend. I waited a minute or two – just to be sure, then crept inside. There was no-one there so I knew they'd gone down the mine.'

Anna was staring at him excitedly, eager to hear more. 'And I'd only come up with them half an hour before,' she said. 'Oh my word! What if they'd followed me back down last Friday? Then I'd have been in serious trouble! You know, I think this is bigger than I first thought!'

'I think you're right Anna and do you know what? I waited and waited, hidden in the dark, expecting them to carry out some inspection or whatever and return but they didn't! I waited until eight o'clock then decided they probably weren't coming back. That's when I gave up and went home.'

They both sat in silence. 'Where do we go from here Mr Williamson?'

'Well Anna, they did not repeat this visit for the rest of the week, so let me keep watch a few weeks longer, to see if there's a pattern in their behaviour. That way at least we can establish when it might be safe for us to take a look for ourselves without being caught out.'

'But what if they're planning something bad? What if we wait too long and some tragedy happens?'

'This has probably been going on for some time Anna. I don't think a couple more weeks will make much difference. Better safe than sorry.' He shook his head, looking troubled. 'I always had my doubts about Harris you know. He's a brutal chap. I wouldn't be surprised if he hasn't struck some sort of bargain with these strangers.'

Anna had to wait three more weeks until Williamson brought her more news. She felt as if she would burst with anticipation and yet she knew he was right – they were better off waiting. Her mind churned over all sorts of likelihoods and possible outcomes but she felt she knew too little to ascertain what was actually going on.

On the third Sunday, after school, Mr Williamson nodded at her. She knew this meant he had more to tell her, so she busied herself tidying the book shelves until the room was clear.

'I was right Anna! The same thing's happened every Monday for the past three weeks. Something's going on down there.'

She nodded enthusiastically for him to continue. Suddenly the expression on his face grew solemn. 'Now Anna, you may not like this, but we've hatched a plan.'

'What do you mean *we*?' she frowned. Surely he hadn't divulged this to anyone else!

He nodded reassuringly. 'Now don't worry. I've worked with and lived amongst these men for over thirty years Anna and I know whom I can and cannot trust. I had to confide in a few of them.'

She gasped.

'Don't worry; I know I've made the right choice. We've decided to do the same thing you did Anna – we're going down on Friday night to see for ourselves.'

'Then I'm coming too!'

He looked kindly at her. 'No Anna. You have been more than brave, and if anything comes of this then it will all be down to you, but I cannot let you take any further risks. I would never forgive myself if you came to harm.'

The disappointment was written all over her face, but inside she knew he was right. She made one last ditch attempt, 'But I'll be safe with all of you!'

'No Anna. I insist. There will be four of us. I promise I will tell you all about it next Sunday but you really must trust me now. You must let me see this through.'

Reluctantly she agreed. 'For goodness sake then be careful and stay safe. I too will never forgive myself if you come to harm.' Her expression was serious. 'And perhaps it's better if you don't tell me the names of the men you've chosen.'

Yet another working week went by uneventfully with Anna barely able to sleep or eat. Her insides churned constantly. She could not wait for Sunday School. But what if Mr Williamson were not there? What if the men came to danger? No – surely she'd hear gossip in the village if anything was amiss. She would just have to be patient.

It was a huge relief to see him at the front of the chapel ready to take the lesson, but she immediately noticed that he looked drawn and read his worried expression. During the hour of teaching he could barely bring himself to glance at her, afraid that his face might give him away. When they were alone he began in a low whisper, his eyes wild. 'You were right Anna! Oh how right you were! It is another world!'

Anna didn't know whether or not to feel relieved. 'So what did you see?'

'Pretty much the same as you. After a while we ventured a short distance from the door. The ground was hard going and the air was permeated with a toxic, sulphurous smell. And the noise!' He put both hands over his ears, full of the memory. 'Oh the sound fills your head with its horrible grinding! We couldn't believe what we were experiencing. All of us were nervous Anna, and trust me, those men are tough! They've experienced enough danger underground over the years, but all of us were pretty terrified!'

'Go on – did you see anything else?' Anna's eyed were round and bright as two full moons.

'Having seen enough and being too scared to explore further we soon headed back. We were concerned as to whether or not the unfamiliar air might harm us. Our lungs felt heavy and a pressure grew inside our chests. Suddenly, just as we reached the door, we heard echoing voices coming towards us from the inside. We had to conceal ourselves quickly behind the rocks.'

'Was it them?' Anna was on the edge of the bench.

'Yes. The door opened and they emerged – Harris, Peningrade and the other four, deep in discussion.'

'What were they saying? I can't believe this! I thought you said they never went there on Fridays! What if they'd seen you?' Full of questions, yet at the same time eager to allow him to complete his tale.

'They spoke in hushed voices but three of us plainly heard Peningrade say to Harris, "Soon. We need to end it very soon. There is nothing left here to sustain us. We need to bring the remainder of our people out soon." Then Harris asked how many were left and Peningrade replied, "Just a few hundred - come and see for yourself." The four others had not opened their mouths. They had merely glanced from one to another, as if they did not understand the conversation. With that they all strode off, Harris clambering in a rather ungainly manner as he attempted to negotiate the sharp rocks of the landscape, the others managing it with relative ease.'

Anna stared, mouth agape.

'They disappeared out of sight and we were undecided as to what we should do. One of our boys said, "Whatever they're planning, they said they are going to do it soon – you heard them, this might be our only chance." The thought spurred us on, so carefully we traced their steps. As we rounded the bend we couldn't believe our eyes!'

'What was it?'

'Anna! There in the ground sat the most enormous hole. It must have been at least a mile in diameter – and it went down deep; so deep in fact that from where we stood we could not see the bottom. It was as though a giant asteroid had exploded on the land. There was no sign of life. In the far distance we could just make out the figures of Harris, Peningrade and the other four as they stood talking, but they were too far away for us to hear any of their conversation.'

He paused and looked at her, as if to see if she was taking it all in before continuing. 'And then the strangest thing happened! We stood half-crouched, peering out from behind the rocks and watched. Shortly after, their conversation ended abruptly. Harris turned and began walking back in our direction as clumsily as before. We knew we could afford to wait a few moments longer as his focus was fixed firmly on the ground beneath his feet – he's not the most graceful of fellows at the best of times!' He grinned. 'Anyway, they watched his back as he walked away, then, once he was a bit of a distance, and just as we were about to turn back ourselves, they suddenly – well, they suddenly changed, right before our very eyes!' He stared into the near distance, as though dis-trustful of his memory.

'What do you mean *changed?*' Anna asked, bringing him back to the moment.

'Well, it was the strangest sight! All at the same time, Peningrade and the other four seemed to shrink – No, not shrink. They grew shorter yes, but not small, just a different shape. I've never seen anything like it Anna. It sounds crazy, I know! Their clothing melted into thin air. Their skin took on a matt, purplish-grey hue and their frames became squared and more muscular as they continued to watch him. We all gasped and looked at each other but could not speak for fear of being heard. No, we stared ahead, our attention away from Harris now and back to them. Their eyes were acidic yellow, almost luminous as they watched him go.' He shivered, recalling the image.

'It's hard to believe – and yet I do believe it; after what I saw myself, I do believe it,' she said. 'But what can we do? What do you think they are up to?'

'The men and I have discussed it Anna, and we believe that whoever they are - whatever they are - they have used up all the resources their land has to offer and are now after ours. We believe, that over the past two years, they have attempted to fuel their world with coal from our mine but are now realizing that it is not enough, and so they have decided to come and inhabit our world instead.'

'But it's incredible! Do you think they might harm us if they come?'

'As a Christian Anna I have wrestled with this thought I can tell you! The thing is they obviously have powers which we ourselves do not possess; after all, there is no-one in our world who can change shape like that is there?'

'Absolutely not!'

'So we must not allow them to come Anna. The men and I have decided that we cannot run the risk of allowing our earth to be overcome by these – these alien beings.'

'But I still do not see what can be done about it!' Anna was afraid now. Her voice trembled as she spoke. She could not even begin to imagine a possible solution.

Mr Williamson looked kindly at her and his excited voice grew gentle. 'Remember when you first trusted me with what you knew?'

'Yes.'

'And you asked me to keep it secret?'

'Yes.'

'Well now I must ask you to keep this secret. Leave it to us Anna. Whatever you hear in the coming days, however hard it might be, and however much you might want to speak of it, you simply must not. You must take this secret to the grave. Do you promise?'

'Well yes of course, but what secret? What do you intend to do?'

His expression was grim. 'I cannot tell you any more Anna, for I do not want you to feel the burden of knowing that you had any part in what is about to happen. Trust me – that is all I ask.'

Returning to work on Monday, Anna was terrified. She could not bear to even glance in the direction of the four miners as they entered the cage. She longed for the blackness of the journey underground.

The carts were hauled back and fore, just as they had always done, but it was strange now, knowing what they were really doing with the load, and more than that, what they intended to do soon.

At 3:00a.m. on Wednesday morning she was jolted out of a deep sleep. There was no mistake! The siren had sounded! The whole house stirred and she heard her dad take the stairs, two at a time. Immediately she leapt out of bed and began to dress. Her mother soon appeared at the door to her bedroom, 'What do you think you are doing? You are not going anywhere!'

'But Mum! I must see for myself!'Anna ducked under her mother's arm and ran down the street to join most of the village. Everyone knew that when the alarm sounded it meant a collapse or an explosion! Lives were in danger, and if they could help then they would; it was what they had all been brought up to do – an unspoken loyalty.

Her stomach was in knots as she approached the mine. People were everywhere, some shouting instructions and names of those who were known to be on night shift. It was all one huge, chaotic scene of panic.

Soon a familiar voice could be heard over the tannoy. There was no mistake – Anna knew that voice too well. It was Mr Williamson. Relief washed over her trembling body. She froze in order to listen, as did most of the others. 'It's fine everyone! It's number two! There's been an explosion in shaft two. The roof's fallen in. No-one was down there – it doesn't operate during night. You have our word that shaft one's fine. Go back to your beds. The team can see if there's anything to be done in the morning when we have light.'

Anna shared the relief of those around her. It was as if they all sighed together at the words. Then a voice in the crowd shouted, 'Where's Harris? No-one's seen him and he's not at home.' A murmur spread through the crowd, though the question did not seem to heighten the panic – Harris had never been the most popular member of the village. In fact, the crowd were already moving en-masse, away from the pit, back towards the narrow little streets.

Anna knew she would receive a ticking off when she got home but she did not care – she had to speak with Mr Williamson. She pushed her way through the crowd, in the opposite direction from which it now flowed. Eventually she spotted him standing on the make-shift platform of an up-turned coal cart, tannoy in hand. He appeared to be in deep discussion with three men. As she approached they turned and looked at her. All four stopped talking and smiled. She did not return the gesture. Her frown fixed on Mr Williamson, who stepped away from them and took her aside.

'What's going on?' she asked breathlessly.

'All you need to know Anna is that it's done. It's ended.'

'But what do you mean? Is anyone hurt? Where's Harris? And what about Peningrade? Were they down there?' She didn't know whether to feel relief or concern; after all, she didn't want to be party to murder!

He held her by the shoulders and looked into her eyes. 'Trust me Anna! It had to be done – for all our sakes and the sakes of those not yet born, it had to be done.' His face was alight with relief. She glanced around and saw the other three men watching them closely. One of them winked at her.

'But are they dead?'

'No Anna, they have simply returned to their world, where they belong. It's just that now they have one more member.' He sighed and glanced away. 'Harris could not be saved. He made his own bed so to speak...

Remember your promise Anna. Take it to the grave!'

Ash

El Golfo, Lanzarote, 1920

Raoul vomited overboard for the third time. The crossing from Morocco had been violent, for it was high summer and the time when the trade winds raged mercilessly. The flimsy little fishing boat, hired at El Aaiun, had thrashed about like a delirious child in the throes of some infernal sickness and clammy, stress-induced perspiration, as well as sea-spray rendered his whole body damp and odorous.

Under normal circumstances public vomiting would have horrified Raoul, but as he was the only passenger and the skipper's full attention was given over to controlling the helm, Raoul largely escaped embarrassment. He did however regret his choice of clothing, for he had lost his boater to the wind within the first ten minutes and his ivory-coloured linen suit now callously displayed dark patches of sweat.

Finally the boat moored at the tiny quay of El Golfo and he was able to vacate the vessel which for the past few hours had attempted to claim his mortal soul. Hands trembling, he was barely able to grasp the rope which hung from the rail and his unstable legs threatened to give way beneath him. Clasping his brown-leather briefcase to his chest, in an effort to hide a vomit stain, he made no attempt to rescue his travelling trunk from the hull. Sympathising somewhat with Raoul's condition the skipper tied the boat firmly and heaved the trunk ashore on his behalf, then with little more than a nod and a quick exchange of pesetas departed back to sea.

The little quay was no more than six feet square and apart from Raoul was unoccupied. He stared despondently at the steep, black path which ascended between the great igneous rocks ahead, wondering how he would ever find the strength to climb it. Due to the weather his journey had taken almost two hours longer than anticipated and he assumed therefore that Father Carlos - who had arranged to meet him - would have by now given up and gone home.

Cricking his neck first left then right in an attempt to relieve the tension and shielding his eyes from the infernal mid-day sun, he peered upwards towards the path's horizon. From where he stood it was just possible to make out the white, rectangular shape of the church and the simple metal cross and bell which stood on its roof.

Due to his current incapacitation he was grateful for the solitude in which to gather himself and so, not wishing to be seen in his present state, slumped down on a rock and, retrieving a clean white handkerchief from his breast pocket, proceeded to mop his brow.

The potent trade wind cooled him rapidly and thus, a few minutes later, he stumbled up the path towards the church. Its brightly-painted blue door stood wide open. Raoul entered without waiting for an invite.

'Ah, Raoul I presume?' The priest shook his hand, smiling, though the tension was visible between his brows. 'I'd given you up as lost at sea!'

'I do apologize father. It was a very rough crossing.'

The priest nodded sympathetically. 'Come! Sit and have a glass of water before I take you home – you seem a little shaken.'

In his letter Father Carlos had insisted that there would be no need for Raoul to seek lodgings and that he would be welcome at his own home. This being Raoul's first visit to Lanzarote, or indeed any of the Canary Islands, meant that he was grateful for the gesture. And so, pleasantries exchanged, some fifteen minutes or so later Raoul found himself ensconced in a stark but pleasantly cool bedroom.

The priest's house was a typical Canarian finca, consisting of a single-storey, flat-roofed cuboid which stood some fifty yards or so away from the little church. A dry, lava rock wall encircled its boundary. No garden to speak of – just a small frontage of crushed lava rock from which grew, as if by some miracle, an impressive array of cacti.

The inside of the house was equally as frugal. Its entrance revealed a narrow, windowless hallway with doors which led to a kitchen-cum-living room, Raoul's bedroom and another to what must presumably be Father Carlos's bedroom.

Raoul picked at the simple plate of grilled fish in front of him, his stomach still queasy from the turbulent journey. 'In the contents of your letter I could sense your urgency Father, and yet - I hope you don't mind me saying - I also felt you were keeping something back. Am I correct in inferring that you have not yet told me the full extent of your concerns?'

'Indeed Raoul. There are many things which I couldn't explain fully in the letter. The intent of my correspondence was to provide you with sufficient detail with which to pique your interest and in doing so hopefully enlist your help. However, I was also mindful of the fact that many of the details of events which have taken place here over the past year would likely appear to a stranger as mere flights of fancy. Indeed, not only do they fly in the face of religion but would also perhaps seem infeasible to all but the crudest of minds! Believe me when I say I have not reached my conclusion fleetingly Raoul. No – it is only after much soul-searching that I can even begin to contemplate that what has occurred might be something other than the ravings of a lunatic.'

'The events you hinted at did indeed stir my interest to say the least Father, but why *me* if you don't mind me asking? Why do you consider the matter a case for an anthropologist rather than the police?'

Father Carlos adjusted his position and leaned closer, as though about to whisper. 'Let me explain from the beginning. I'm sure you will then understand why I believe *you* are the best person to help.'

Raoul gestured with open hands for the priest to enlighten him.

'May I begin by familiarizing you a little with the history of our island and its people? I believe it might help you to recognize that what is happening here now is somehow linked to the past.'

'Yes of course.'

'Well in that case I shall begin by explaining about the ground upon which our church is built. The site was originally a shrine, first built in the early part of the 17th century in the form of a small, dome-shaped, structure. It was built by the Catholic Church to honour the Senora de la Caridad but was destroyed during the great Timanfaya eruption of 1730.' He sighed loudly. 'The important thing is that it was *unburied* just ten or so years ago, around 1909, and the shrine was subsequently incorporated into the little church you see today. The Catholic Church always attempts to include as much of the heritage of the island as it can when it builds.'

He paused and studied Raoul's face for a moment. 'You see, during the 15th century, this island was embroiled in the slave trade from North Africa. Under Spanish control, many slaves were captured in order to help populate the island. Then, during the 16th century, Moorish pirates attacked the island in retaliation and took back slaves of their own.

However, it is my knowledge of what occurred on this island prior to all of this which is part of the reason why I seek your help; it is the connection between recent events and events of long ago, before ever this island was under

Spanish rule, which most concern me.'

Father Carlos paused again to ensure he had Raoul's full attention, before looking him straight in the eye and continuing in an unsteady voice. 'It is alleged that the society of this island at the time was polygamous with each woman taking three husbands. It is thought that this custom may have been a consequence of female infanticide, practised to limit the population on such an arid island with extremely limited resources. So you see – your knowledge of anthropology is of value.'

Raoul appeared thoughtful. His face flushed a little by the wine, he urged the priest to continue. 'Tell me Father exactly when did the first infant disappear?'

'Just less than thirteen months ago Raoul. The first victim was a baby girl, just three months old, and the first-born child to her parents. I baptised her on Sunday 18th of August. Look, here I have the Register of Births, Deaths and Marriages from the church.'

The priest opened a large tome to where a gold-ribboned page marker lay in wait. 'See here?' he said pointing. 'It says, *Maria Juanita Sanchez - female - born 29th July 1919 at El Golfo to parents Marisa and Juan Sanchez. Father - farm labourer.*'

Raoul studied the handwritten font and confirmed the priest's words with a nod.

'The baptism was a typical, simple affair. The family held a little celebration back at their home, to which I was invited, as is the custom. All were happy and content and I detected so sign from any of the guests that anything was amiss.

'However, having put the infant to sleep in her crib beside their own bed and having fallen contentedly to sleep themselves, at around 2 o'clock in the morning, an intense heat caused Marisa to wake. She initially assumed it to be hormonal. Her heart was palpitating and she was soaked in perspiration.

'Within a few seconds she believed she could detect a faint smell of burning and instinctively reached out her hand towards baby Maria's crib. Her hand failed to locate the child's presence. She assumed, that having had a tiring day, she must have slept through the baby's cry and that her husband had taken the infant into his side of the bed. She stressed that this had never happened before as she was in tune to the baby's every breath. Anxiously she reached across her sleeping husband and patted the small space of mattress. When baby Maria was not there she shouted for her husband to wake up. He himself had consumed a few glasses of wine during the afternoon celebration but had in no way been drunk.'

Raoul's interest was piqued as he awaited the outcome of the story.

'Fumbling to light the lamp on her bedside table, her hand brushed against the tiny St. Christopher which had been given to her baby daughter as a gift that very afternoon by her grandmother. Marisa had carefully removed it from her sleeping daughter's delicate neck before placing her in the crib, in case it should harm the child in her sleep. She swears, that even though her fingers only fleetingly brushed against it, the metal was hot as coals! Quickly withdrawing her hand, she heard it fall to the floor. She says it was then that she *just knew* that her baby was dead. She screamed, waking her husband.

'Of course, as I informed you in my letter Raoul, the baby was nowhere to be found. The local policía attended within the hour but, despite a wide investigation, no crime could be confirmed. The whole area was searched, witnesses interviewed and the baby's crib was sent to the mainland for forensic investigation. Meanwhile I myself was interviewed and I do believe that for a while even I was suspected of having somehow harmed the child.'

Raoul could sense the desperation in the priest's eyes. 'And what was the outcome of the forensics Father?'

'It was in fact the examination of the crib which led to the only clue as to what might have happened to baby Maria. Traces of sulphurous ash were detected amongst the fabric of the infant's blanket. Yet the fabric was neither burnt nor scorched. Some of the ash contained the tiniest traces of human D.N.A., so tiny in fact that it would have borne little weight as evidence in a trial.'

'You say *some* of the ash. What do you mean by some?'

'The forensic report claimed that *two* types of ash were present; the one I have mentioned but also ash which seemed to have derived from an organic source other than human. This second type of ash contained trace elements of sulphur, as if it had derived from the bowels of the volcano. This could neither be explained by the forensic scientists nor the policía and the case was merely left open. Poor Marisa and Juan had no body to bury and no answer as to the disappearance of their beautiful baby.'

The light in the priest's living room seemed to dim abruptly. Both aware of it at the same time, Father Carlos stood stiffly and lit several candles which were waiting on various receptacles and ledges around the room. Raoul took another sip of the somewhat course but never the less calming wine and contemplated what he had just heard. Fingers folded and pressed to his chin he awaited the priest's return to the table.

'So it is your belief that there is a link between the recent occurrence of the baby girl's disappearance and an ancient, though not proven custom,' he said, a deep-set frown upon his face.

'I do. Against my better judgement I do indeed. Believe me Raoul the idea comes to me as a last resort. You see, as a solitary event, Baby Maria's loss would have been bad enough, but since then another three babies have disappeared on this part of the island in almost exact same circumstances. All have been female and all were baptised by my own hands at the little church in which we met earlier today.'

Roaul exhaled rather noisily. 'Have you baptised any male infants here since the baby's disappearance Father?'

'Yes. Two. Both of whom remain unharmed.' Father Carlos glanced fleetingly at Raoul. 'During the past three months, no parent has brought their newborn to me for fear it might happen again. Can you imagine how this makes me feel Raoul? *I* know I am totally innocent of having anything to do with this horrendous crime and yet I cannot blame my flock for losing faith. Now do you see why I wished to tell you this in person rather than in a letter?'

'Most certainly! So tell me Father, where exactly do your own suspicions lie?'

A small whimper emitted from the priest's throat. 'Oh Raoul! This is where I fear you will think me mad. I have spoken of my suspicions to no-one else. I had to turn to someone, I am desperate! Do you understand?'

'Of course. Believe me Father, I am not here to judge your thoughts or actions. Over the past twenty years, during my journeys throughout the world, I have been called upon to consider numerous strange and unexplained happenings, many of which could not be explained through science. Now, even though I am trained to think and act scientifically, I always begin with an open mind. Like you I too believe there are influences that reach beyond mankind, though I will tell you here and now - so that there is no misunderstanding between us Father- my belief in a religious God differs from your own.'

'I am grateful Raoul. For a priest to question his own faith is a terrible thing. However, what I have witnessed this past year has indeed made me doubt that we humans hold the answer to the root of mankind's presence on this earth though I would not of course speak these thoughts publicly. So, to return to your question regarding my own suspicions Raoul, I fear that whatever is taking these poor, innocent souls may have something to do with a *force* connected to the time when the people of this island practised infanticide. I am even beginning to question whether or not there may be a discrepancy between what the suggested purpose of this infanticide was - namely that of limiting the island's population - and what the real reason might have been.'

'Are you suggesting that the practise of infanticide was carried out merely as an evil act? Perhaps pagan in nature?'

Father Carlos paled and wrung his hands with the discomfort of admitting his thoughts. 'In a way pagan yes, but not evil; at least not evil on the part of those forced to carry out the sacrifices. I believe, against my better judgement, that some *power* - I know not what - demanded the sacrifices in return for allowing the islanders to remain safe.'

Raoul looked perplexed. 'Explain Father. What has led you to hold such thoughts?'

'Unorthodox as it sounds, I wonder if some presence within the volcano itself demanded sacrifices be made in return for it remaining inactive.' Father Carlos looked away from Raoul as he said this, all too aware of how it sounded.

Silence ensued, during which time the priest stared forlornly at his feet, as does a man condemned.

Raoul was first to break the silence. 'Apart from the traces of ash found during the forensics do you have any other physical evidence to justify such claims Father?'

'Very few, yet enough to have led me to form my judgement.'

'And they are..?'

'Well, there was no other evidence from the first disappearance. However, following the second baby's disappearance, my instincts were on high alert and so I carried out a painstaking examination of the church. Indeed, not only did I find traces of ash, albeit minute ones, leading from the door of the crypt to the church entrance, but I also found scorch marks on both doors which I'm certain were not there previously. Look I photographed and dated them as carefully as I could.'

Father Carlos stood, and unlocking a small bureau in the corner of the room, retrieved a brown envelope which he placed in front of Raoul. The contents of the envelope revealed several photographs of the two doors. Raoul examined them carefully. Indeed, each showed marks which appeared like scorches.

'Did you point out the traces of ash and these marks to the police?' Raoul asked.

'I did not. I was afraid that it would only convince them that I was indeed connected to the crime and besides, by then I had formed other ideas in my mind which suggested to me that this was not a crime committed by humans.'

'Go on.'

'Well, do you see? If my suggestion is correct, and there is indeed some presence within the bowels of the volcano demanding human flesh, then it may be that as the Europeans gained control of the island and made the established religion one of Catholicism, the sacrifices by the indigenous people ceased. Therefore, the presence was not *fed*. Angry at not have its demands met it retaliated by causing the great volcanic eruption of Timanfaya in 1730 which destroyed much of the island.'

Raoul struggled to prevent the doubt he was feeling from showing in his face. 'But what about since? I'm not saying I don't believe your trail of thought Father, but the eruption occurred almost two hundred year ago. If what you say is true, surely whatever *it* was wouldn't have waited this long to act again!'

The priest stood abruptly and banged his fists on the table, causing Raoul to visibly flinch. 'Don't think I haven't had the same doubts Raoul. Believe me   for a man who has spent almost his entire life believing that there is only one God and that only He can create or take life it is not an idea that sits comfortably with me!'

Somewhat breathless from his outburst, he slumped back down heavily. 'You see, the great eruption of the 1730's was not the only one. Since then there have been several others, albeit less significant ones. But what has really aroused my suspicion is the fact that the Shrine of la Caridad remained buried in lava and therefore closed, so to speak, for the best part of two hundred years. It seems to me more than coincidence therefore, that it being re-discovered and therefore unburied ten years ago, has once again coincided with the disappearance of female infants.'

'But what do you mean *closed*? What exactly was opened by the church being built on the site of the shrine? And is there even any connection between the shrine and a place of sacrifice?' Raoul shook his head. 'I don't wish to seem unconvinced Father but unlike you I am struggling to make the links at present.'

The priest bit his bottom lip. 'I told you earlier Raoul, the church was not just built on top of a site where a shrine once stood; the shrine was actually unburied and therefore re-opened. After being suffocated, so to speak, by solidified lava for two hundred years, the shrine at the head of the ancient cave system could once again breathe. This island is riddled with cave systems which lead from its volcanoes to the sea and is referred to locally as *The Badlands* perhaps not without good reason.

He paused to gather his breath. 'A crypt lies beneath the church and forms part of a cave system here. It may be impassable in places and I have never attempted to explore it. This particular cave system eventually emerges at Los Hervideros, or *boiling waters*. I believe that the evil presence I speak of originates in the bowels of the volcano and travels around the island in its lust to consume pure, infant souls for the simple reason that it developed a taste for the same in the past!' His eyes were aflame with passion. When Raoul didn't interject he continued. 'I believe that the Shrine of La Caridid was built on an ancient sacrificial site and that in unburying the shrine, and thereby re-opening the entrance to the cave, this evil has once again reignited its lust for human flesh!' Father Carlos leaned back in the chair, spent.

When Raoul still did not speak the priest implored him. 'Please Raoul. You are my last hope! I'm not saying I've got it exactly right but do you think it is possible that there is some evil force at work here? Some force other than a human kind?'

'Father, I acknowledge that what has occurred over the last year cannot easily be explained and that you have indeed uncovered some very strange facts. However, I have to tell you that for the present I remain open-minded.' Raoul read the look of despondency on Father Carlos's face and pitied him. 'Are you a fit man? Do you think that tomorrow, after we have examined the church together, we might examine the crypt and even the cave?'

The gesture cheered the priest somewhat. 'Indeed Raoul! I must admit that I have not been brave enough thus far to explore it alone but in your company I would feel more confident. For now though I think we both need an early night. Would you agree?'

*

Despite a fitful night's sleep, Raoul and the priest were up at the crack of dawn and soon afterwards made their way to the little church. As they walked they shared mere pleasantries, the intense discussion of the previous evening for now a mute, unwelcome companion. Once inside though it could no longer be ignored.

'Is the church door locked at night Father?'

'Always Raoul, and since the disappearance of the first victim I have checked it carefully.'

'And does anyone else hold a key?'

'No. I am the sole key holder.' He passed the sturdy, metal object to Raoul. 'See for yourself. It would not be possible for anyone or indeed any *thing* to open the door without the key.'

Raoul nodded in agreement. 'And on the mornings following the victims' disappearance, are you certain that the church remained locked?'

'Absolutely! As I explained last night, the only evidence of disturbance relating to the door are the scorch marks which you can see for yourself.'

Raoul cast his gaze around the nave and pointed. 'And what about the little window?'

'I have not examined the window Raoul. It is too high to reach without a ladder.'

'Would you mind if I moved the altar table and climbed up to take a look?'

'Be my guest; I'm sure the Lord will not take offence if it means us helping his servants.' Father Carlos smiled weakly, though his eyes remained cheerless.

Clearing the table of its contents, they dragged the heavy oak slab over to the little window. Raoul removed his spectacles and instead held a magnifying glass to his eye. The priest watching anxiously from below.

'Do you think you could climb up Father? I'm almost certain there are scorch marks on the wood here.'

Father Carlos did as requested. Indeed, the scorch marks around the bottom of the window were significant.

'I assume it has been a while since the window itself was opened?'

'I have been resident here for nine years and have never needed to open it Raoul. In fact, until now, I wasn't even aware that it had a catch.'

'Then it will likely be stiff. Let's see— ' Raoul lifted the metal catch from its keeper and turned it towards him. The window gave with surprising ease. A sudden breeze blew sharply, taking them both by surprise. 'No reluctance there!' Raoul said before examining the catch with the same magnifier. Indeed, the once white paint was missing in places and the bare metal was tinged a brownish-blue as though it had been heated.

'Strange! Is there anything we can use to climb up and examine the window from the outside?' he asked the priest.

'No. But I can walk over to Sanchez's farm if you like and ask to borrow a ladder. It should only take ten minutes or so.'

'Alright. But try not to arouse suspicion. I think it best if just the two of us look for the present. Do you think you can avoid him offering to bring it here for you?'

'Yes I think so. Old Sanchez is likely out working his vines at this time of morning and I doubt the Senora will offer to carry it. She's well in her 70's! If she asks, I'll tell her I fear there is a leak in the roof.'

Once Father Carlos had gone Raoul propped open the window, rejoicing in the breeze, before again climbing down. He walked over to the door to the crypt. It appeared exactly as it had done in the photos. The scorch marks were evident. There were four in total, each in a different place, but all approximately at waist height. Around the height where hands might push, Raoul thought, though he acknowledged no hand-like shape to the marks. Half expecting the door to be locked, he grasped the metal handle and turned. It relented with little more than a creak.

Retrieving a torch from his briefcase, he shone the beam into the pitch-black void. Opening the door wide, he propped it open with a hymn book and stepped inside. After the relative warmth of the church, its cold, dank air sent a chill down his spine. Shining the torch around the sloping walls, he saw that the crypt was empty. A faint trickle of water could be heard in the distance. Raoul could see that this part of the church was indeed formed from a cave, just as the priest had said. The roof sloped away quite sharply, as did the floor, and following the route with his torch, he saw that it continued into the visible distance. Raoul shivered, both from cold and excitement.

Reluctant at present to examine the depths of the cave, he returned to the door and once again shone the torch around the walls. He thought it similar to the inside of a coal mine; the walls perspired, black and shiny, the pattern of stratified lava rippling like waves. Raoul could picture the sea cooling and calming the flow of molten lava, hushing and caressing, as would a mother soothing a child's temper. Reluctant to shut the door in order to examine it from inside at present, he simply breathed in the coolness of the air. It had always surprised him that a cave should remain at such a constant temperature and be so suddenly in opposition to its neighbouring environment. He closed his eyes for a moment and focussed on the distant sound of water...

'Where are you Raoul?' The priest's return jolted him back to the present.

*

Having both agreed that there were indeed scorch marks around the outside of the window frame, Raoul and the priest returned to the crypt. This time they lit a gas lamp, which Father Carlos suspended from the ceiling of the cave, then closed the door behind them so that they could examine its interior surface.

Once again a series of marks were located, though as the interior of the crypt door was of dark wood they were less obvious and mostly detectable by touch. Gouges, approximately a quarter of an inch deep, scarred the wood. These gouges were linear in shape as if whatever had caused them had scratched at the door, rather as might a pet wishing to enter.

Raoul followed the shape of the gouges with his own finger nails but the pattern did not match in the slightest. If a human hand had scraped at the door one would expect three lines of demarcation. Additionally, the depth of the second gouge would likely be deepest due to the middle finger being the longest.

There were two detectable sets of gouges on the inside of this door, running almost parallel to one another. Each set of marks bore six vertical lines, approximately two feet in length which ran from Raoul's head height to his waist. On the left side, the sixth mark was gouged deeper than the others and on the right side the reverse was true. If indeed these marks had been caused by some *being* scraping at the door it would suggest that it had two hands, each with six fingers, not allowing for a thumb, its index finger being the longest.

'I noticed whilst you were away that this door was unlocked,' Raoul said. 'Is this usual?'

'Yes. In fact, if you observe, this door has no key-hole. I have never found it necessary to install a lock as only rarely is the church open without me being present.'

'Then if some *being* tried to enter from the cave, it would not have been necessary for it to scratch at the door in this way would it Father?'

'No, I suppose not.' They stared at the door, puzzled.

'Unless—' continued Raoul, 'Whatever it was did not

have the kind of extremities which might allow it to grasp and turn a handle?'

Father Carlos nodded. 'Why do you suppose it would have scratched at both the left and right sides of the door Raoul? The handle is in an obvious position.'

'Obvious to us Father, but a non-human entity might have no understanding of what a door entails never mind a door handle! Nor would it have been able to see a door in the pitch dark of the crypt, assuming *it* even had sense of sight! If something was journeying along this cave, with the intention of entering the island, it would merely have experienced the door as an obstacle in its path.'

Both men wore a puzzled frown.

'Shall we return home for lunch and attempt to piece together what we have found thus far?' asked the priest. 'We could return at around six thirty when it is cooler outside. We would still have at least three hours of daylight.'

*

'If your suppositions are correct Father, how do you suppose an evil presence, or whatever you might call it, could possibly have known about the baptisms? I mean, we can be certain that it could not possibly have any understanding of the ceremony of religion can it? Are you certain that no female babies, apart from those you baptised, have been harmed?'

'Of course I'm certain! Do you not think that another disappearance would have gone unreported! Why, I do believe there isn't a soul on these islands, or indeed the mainland, who isn't aware of what has happened here!' Father Carlos answered, his voice raised in frustration.

'Don't get angry Father. I am merely trying to determine the facts. I do not want us to leave out any piece of the puzzle. It's just that I cannot begin to comprehend why such a being would choose the babies baptised at this church in particular, nor can I believe that it has chosen souls who have been welcomed that very day into the arms of the Lord. I mean it's ridiculous! It makes it seem as if the *thing* is intelligent!'

'If I knew the answers to your questions Raoul then I would have had no need to enlist your help! I have gone over and over these same questions in my mind time and time again this past year. All I know is that somehow this *thing* is preying on female babies fresh from their baptism here and is mocking us in doing so!'

'I agree Father, but unless we find more evidence I cannot begin to comprehend the how or why.'

*

'I think we should put off exploring the cave itself until tomorrow. We'll start afresh early in the morning if you agree.'

Both men had returned to the church that same evening and having re-examined the whole of its interior had found no further clues. The task had not taken more than an hour or so, as the simple rectangular building had few nooks and crannies to uncover.

'I do indeed Father but as we have about another hour of daylight shall we return to the crypt for another look? Let us light the extra lanterns we brought.'

Raoul shivered and slipped on his jacket as he entered the crypt. Father Carlos set about positioning the lanterns at various points. Eerie shadows danced around the black walls. 'It would be easy to allow one's imagination to get the better of one Father, do you not think?' Raoul grinned at the priest.

'Most certainly Raoul! So let us focus on the job with an unemotional mind. I've had enough of allowing my imagination to get the better of me.'

'The water sounds louder this evening Father.'

'It is high tide at Los Hervidores at this time of day Raoul. I must take you to see it one day. The way the water races in and out of the mouths of the lava tunnels is incredible! It is little wonder that it is known locally as the boiling point.'

'I would like to see it Father, perhaps tomorrow evening after we have examined the cave here?'

A few minutes passed in silence, both Raoul and the priest examining the walls of the cave.

'Raoul— Come and look at this! Do you see what I see?'

Raoul approached the section of wall just to the right of the crypt door where Father Carlos stood squinting.

'Here Raoul! Shine the torch here!'

Raoul shone the beam towards where the priest pointed. It was difficult to make out as the walls reflected the marks with their dampness, but yes on close inspection it was just possible to make out four more gouges. They did not follow the creases and crevices of the rock. Instead, they had almost certainly been carved into the wall by something sharp. 'I see it Father, and I feel it too here, run your fingers along the marks!'

'Do you think it may be of relevance Raoul?'

'It's difficult to say. It could possibly have been the work of whoever installed the door. Let's photograph it to add to your collection.'

The continuous ebb and flow of the distant tide, as it whirled in and out of one lava tube after another, was beginning to consume Raoul's senses, rendering him exhausted. He yawned. 'Shall we call it a day Father? You know, I don't think I've quite recovered from that horrendous journey yesterday. I apologize if I've seemed a little irritable at times.'

The evening sun warmed their shoulders as they strolled the fifty or so yards back to the finca, both deep in thought. Even the winds had ceased. The low sun, bid its final farewell for the day, behind the blackness of Timanfaya.

'The calm before the storm do you think Roaul?' The priest smiled. 'Has what we've found today convinced you in some small way that I may be right?'

'To be honest Father, I'm still not sure. I think I may be more confused now than I was yesterday.'

The simple, evening meal was consumed outdoors and washed down with a half bottle of red wine. The conversation was amicable, during which both priest and anthropologist attempted to turn their thoughts away from recent events. Instead, both took turns to reminisce on past experiences, each man attempting to allow the other to gain a greater awareness of the workings of his individual mind.

*

The following day dawned cloudless and hot as usual. For the time being the winds remained calm. Raoul met the priest in the little kitchen at 7:00a.m.

'Morning Raoul. I was thinking perhaps the four scratch marks that we found engraved in the wall yesterday are a kind of *tally* of its victims, do you think?'

'Possibly Father.' Raoul stifled a yawn.

'We'll need to dress sensibly today if we are to explore the cave. I have two pair of Wellington boots. What size do you take?'

'Size nine Father.'

'Well they're a ten but I'm sure they'll do. You can always don a few pair of socks.'

*

By 8:30, both priest and scientist were ankle deep in water. Each had fastened a crude headlamp, by means of a small torch strapped around the head with a length of old bandage. A small bag, containing additional lanterns, a bottle of water and a notebook was tied around Raoul's neck with a long shoe-lace.

Raoul led the way. For the first ten minutes the cave was easily navigated – all that was required was a little crouching in parts. Now the going was slow. The passageway was only wide enough for one man at a time but thus far the floor had been quite dry. However, during the last minute or two, Raoul had become more and more aware of the sound of the water, and as the walls changed from a glistening damp to a light trickle, the ground beneath them grew more and more wet. It was slippery underfoot and the combination of the narrow passageway and lack of head height rendered both men sore. Raoul, being the taller of the two, had bumped his head on the roof of the cave several times and cursed himself for attempting the journey without some kind of head protection. In addition there had been little to discover so far as the route had merely consisted of stumbling along a downward-sloping passageway. Apart from shining his torch along the walls every few yards or so, there had been little exploring to do. Raoul was beginning to think that they were indeed both mad!

All of a sudden the passageway curved sharply to the left and the sound of water grew louder. Within seconds Raoul and the priest found themselves in a chamber. Here the height of the cave roof was approximately ten feet and it was wonderful to finally be able to stand tall.

The chamber opened out to a circular shape, roughly thirty feet in diameter. An uneven ledge wrapped around three quarters of its circumference which it was possible to walk along. The centre of the floor however contained a deep, dark, swirling pool of water which seemed to flow around a bend in the direction of yet another passageway.

Raoul followed the ledge around the circumference and peered in the direction of the bend. He could see that as the passageway narrowed abruptly, the water from the chamber pool was forced into it quite quickly, forming a kind of fast-flowing stream.

Father Carlos stood close to the entrance to the chamber, seemingly gasping for breath.

'Let's rest here a while,' suggested Raoul. 'To be honest I'm not sure we can travel any further anyway. The speed of the water ahead looks quite dangerous. The passage seems very low and narrow.'

Both men sat on the wet ledge, glad of the rest and contemplated what, if anything, they might do next.

'How deep do you think this pool is Raoul?' asked the priest, gazing into its dark, reflective face.

Raoul lay flat on his front and reached into the water. 'I can just about touch the bottom here. The floor feels very smooth but I think it slopes away in the centre. I imagine it's much deeper there.'

They sat in silence, re-gaining their strength, until their breathing returned to normal. The sound of the water swirling in the pool, before forcing its way around the chamber bend, along with the persistent trickling from roof to floor drowned out all other sound. Raoul shivered in the cold – soaked through and miserable.

Father Carlos shone his torch around the walls of the chamber in both directions and at various heights looking for clues. The walls hinted at nothing. After a few moments he stood and repeated the task, this time traversing slowly on foot as he did so.

Raoul stared into the pool feeling defeated. He began to wonder if indeed this whole investigation was a fool's errand, and whether it was just possible that the priest might even know something he was not admitting to.

Suddenly the feint beam from his lamp caught sight of something glistening in the water. As Raoul moved his head to get a better look, the glisten was lost.

'Can you bring that torch over here Father?' he called. 'I think there's something in the water.'

It took a minute or so for the torch beam to re-locate the object, but the distortion caused by the swirling water meant that it could not be identified as any one thing in particular. It seemed to lie approximately six feet in from the ledge and as such was out of reach. Raoul shifted onto his front once again. He was, by now, so wet that he considered an extra soaking would make little difference. However he was reluctant to wade into the pool for fear of dislodging the object. 'Hold on to my feet Father. I'll see if I can reach it.' The priest gripped firmly. On the third attempt, Raoul's right hand withdrew from the pool, gripping something small and bright.

'What is it Raoul?' The priest's eyes shone bright with anticipation.

Raoul lay the object flat in the palm of his right hand. It was a small, oval band of gold – about the size of a baby's wrist. He shone the torch around its edge. The gold was engraved with a simple, linear pattern. 'I do believe it's a baby's bracelet Father. We may have something here!'

'Dear God, please say it is so,' muttered the priest still on his knees.

Raoul studied the bracelet's inner rim. Suddenly he paused and squinted in the beam of the torch. 'What were the names of the other three victims Father?'

'Louisa Marquez, Phillipa Fernandez and Catalina Diez,' replied the priest without hesitation.

'Look! Here– ' Raoul pointed the narrow beam at the inner rim and held it as still as he possibly could. There was no mistake. The rim was engraved with the initials *C.D.* followed by the words, *May God keep you safe always.*

The priest slapped his knees triumphantly. 'That's it Raoul! Whatever it was that took the infants brought them here! This might mean the bodies are in the pool!'

'Quite possibly – but I do not think we should search the pool ourselves. There is no way of accurately determining its depth and in any case we are ill prepared.'

'Then we shall return tomorrow,' said Father Carlos. 'We will gather everything we need.' His hands were folded, as though in prayer. 'In the name of God I do not know if I wish the bodies to be found here or not! On the one hand the parents would have answers and a grave to visit – but on the other hand...'

Raoul raised out a hand in protest. 'I'm not sure it's the right thing to do Father. Maybe now is the time to recall the police. I mean, we have new evidence here. This search needs to be carried out professionally.'

The priest froze. 'No Raoul! Do you not see that it might implicate me further? What answer could I give them as to why I found it necessary to search this cave?'

'But what if we do find bodies here Father? What will you do then? You cannot pretend they were found elsewhere!' Raoul's voice was stern.

Father Carlos gathered himself. 'I promise you Raoul. We will return fully equipped tomorrow and if indeed we find anything more then we will summon the policía. At least then I will have you with me to confirm my explanations. If we find nothing, then how might I explain the victim's bracelet being in my possession?'

Father Carlos's eyes shone bright in desperation. Raoul could see the anguish in his face. He was unshaven and appeared suddenly old. Raoul felt a surge of pity.

'Alright Father. We will do as you suggest. But you must promise me that if we do find anything further tomorrow, then we will act in accordance with the law.'

'You have my word Raoul. I swear to God above, you have my word!'

The planned excursion to Los Hervideros was postponed that evening, both men too exhausted and anxious as to what the following day might bring to consider sight-seeing.

*

Raoul slept fitfully for most of the night. However, towards dawn, he seemed to sleep more restfully and consequently, by the time he was up and dressed, Father Carlos was already breakfasted and awaiting him in the little garden.

'Ah, Raoul! I'm glad you're up. I'm afraid that I have to go out for a while. One of my parishioners has just called to say that his mother sadly passed during the night so I must go and visit the family to offer my condolences. They are regulars at my church you see.'

'I'm sorry Father. I must have slept on. I didn't even hear your visitor.'

'No, no! Not to worry. I saw him approaching down the track so I went out to greet him. I suspected he might bear sad news; his mother had been quite ill for some time. He didn't want to come in said he had to get back to make arrangements.' He paused. 'I shouldn't be too long, only I know we'd intended an early start. You go ahead and I'll catch up with you soon. Perhaps you could make your way to the chamber and have a better look at the walls and ledge in case we missed any clues. Make no attempt to enter the pool until I arrive though. It might be unsafe.'

Raoul laughed. 'Don't worry Father. I have absolutely no intention of going in that water alone. I will do as you say though. I think that I should carry out a more careful examination of the walls in the narrowest parts of the passageway through which we passed yesterday. If indeed something or someone did carry a baby along that passage it would not have been an easy journey. They would likely have at least left behind some scuff marks, or may even have dropped some other small clue along the way.

121

Raoul was uncertain as to why, but today's journey into the cave seemed even colder than the previous one. Even though he wore two layers of clothing beneath his raincoat his whole body trembled. He considered it was likely a combination of what the search of the pool might bear and the fact that, at least for now, he was alone. He was aware of the pulsing of his own heart beat and the blood pounding in his ears. It seemed even to drown out the sound of the water.

His progress along the passageway was slow. With a degree of precision, he ran the torch beam over the surface of the black, smooth walls as he journeyed, part of him hoping to find further evidence and part of him not wanting to reach the cavern too far ahead of the priest. The thought of entering the whirling, freezing water and worse still any offering it may surrender to him, was not a thought he relished. Yes, he had of course examined corpses as part of his work as an anthropologist but on such occasions he had been able to completely detach any emotional state of mind. He had felt no connection to the person who had once lived and breathed and instead had regarded the corpses of varying ages and stages of decay almost as one would a shop-window mannequin.

For some reason though, the thought of discovering an infant body in the water filled him with dread. Was it because of the information told to him by the priest the previous evening regarding baby Catalina's family? He could not be certain. All that he did know, was that were it not for the priest's obvious despair, he would now be at the police station in Teguise handing over the bracelet.

After about thirty excruciating minutes he reached the cavern without having found even the smallest trace of evidence. Father Carlos would not be long behind he assumed; after all, he himself had started out a fair while after the priest had left to pay his respects to the bereaved family.

Raoul sat on the ledge, close to the spot where the bracelet had been found. The beam from his headlamp bounced off the shiny, black surface of the drenched walls and the water in the pool swirled even more violently than it had done the previous day. Still it had rained during the night a sudden, thunderous deluge which had ceased as abruptly as it had begun. This, Raoul assumed correctly, was the reason why the pool appeared more aggressive this morning.

Now he was alone he was sure he could hear the sea in the distance and wondered how much further it would travel before the mouth of the cave would spew into the boiling point at Los Hervidores.

Time passed by slowly. Glancing at his watch, he saw that he had only been sitting for six or seven minutes but it had seemed much longer. Having carried a sturdier bag bearing more contraptions today, he decided that he would prepare for his descent into the pool rather than wait for the priest; then they would be ready to press ahead with the search as soon as Father Carlos arrived. He did not wish to spend any more time in this God-forsaken place than was absolutely necessary.

Unpacking a metal stake retrieved from the churchyard, a hammer and rope, he proceeded to secure the stake into the ledge at the place which had surrendered the bracelet. The rhythmic banging echoed around the cavern walls, emitting an excruciating volume.

His first attempt failed. Realising that the spot he had chosen could not be hit with sufficient force from the chosen angle he decided to try again higher up, this time by kneeling solidly on the ledge whilst hammering into the cavern wall.

Success! The stake seemed secure. He believed he was

almost temporarily deafened by the resounding clang of metal on rock but felt a brief wave of gratification.

It was just as he was securing the rope to the stake that he first felt the heat. For a fleeting moment he assumed that his body temperature had simply risen from the exertion but realized with seconds that this was not the case. The perspiration on his back suddenly evaporated from what could only be described as a blast of hot air. The hair on his forearms stood on end as slowly he turned to face the water...

It emerged from the depths, seeming to form its own shape as it did so. Raoul, frozen to the spot, stared in disbelief as the towering, black presence rose before him; its powerful, obsidian outline visible even against the black of the cave. Opaquely black - as was the priest's cloak - and yet at the same time its fiery veins oozed a sulphurous liquid which filled Raoul's nostrils, stung his dry throat and permeated the air with its bitter, acrid stench.

As Raoul knelt transfixed the liquid congealed, changing the *thing's* shape again. Its eyes of conflagration bore into Raoul as it approached. No sound did it emit, other than a continuous gurgling. Molten lava spewed from its body, seeming to open up writhing, gaping wounds in its black flesh in doing so.

Momentarily, each wound gaped open to reveal blood-red veins of fire which in turn spewed sulphur. It was no more than two or three feet away now and Raoul could smell his own flesh singeing in the heat...

*

The skipper moored the boat and emerged onto the black pathway. The man was not there as arranged, though it was precisely two o'clock. Hoping not to have come all this way for no reward, he proceeded to climb the steep, black path which rose sharply ahead towards the church. He found the door wide open and so he stepped inside.

'Hola!'

Almost immediately the priest appeared, smiling. 'Aah! You have come for Raoul? I'm afraid he was called away as a matter of urgency two days ago. He had no means of getting a message to you and so he asked me to pay you handsomely by means of apology for your troubles.'

The priest handed the skipper a small, leather purse which bulged hopefully.

The skipper muttered his thanks and turned to leave, slightly peeved that he had made the journey unnecessarily but at the same time hopeful that the contents of the purse would make it worth his while; after all, the man had not been the easiest of passengers he'd obviously had no sea legs!

Bending low, so as to avoid bumping his head on the door of the church, he froze. The priest had again called to him.

'Do you by any chance have a daughter?'

'I do,' replied the skipper proudly, 'and she is soon due to have a baby of her own!'

'Then give her this with my blessing.' He pressed a small, gold bracelet into the man's palm. 'Tell her it will bring the baby good fortune.'

Wave

In Japanese mythology the giant catfish Namazu is the creator of earthquakes. It disturbs the earth by vigorously moving its tail. Many believe that its motive for doing so is in retribution for human greed and in its efforts to redistribute wealth amongst the population.

March 9th 2011, 1:30a.m.

Marsha Cole neatly replaced the duty free magazine in its pocket for the fourth time, just as the heavily accented voice of the stewardess announced ten minutes to landing. She did not need to re-fasten her seat belt as she rarely undid it during flights except when desperate to visit the rest-room. She was a nervous flyer. It was one of the few down sides of her job. No matter how frequently her work took her away from home, her mind refused to accept air travel as the safest form of transport.

As the plane began its descent she peered through heavy-lidded eyes at Tokyo's night sky, focussing beyond the pale, fatigued reflection of her own face towards the multi-coloured illuminations of the city. They twinkled in the distance, reminding her for a moment of what she still thought of as home – Las Vegas, that god-damned twilight zone where wealth reigned.

Still, she had so many good memories of growing up there on the outskirts of the strip, where she and her brother had been raised by a decent mom and dad, whose main concern in life had been the welfare of their two children who simply must be given the opportunity for a better life than what they'd had.

The stewardess flashed her a brief smile from where she too sat buckled in preparation for landing. Immaculate

French-polished nails, slender legs crossed at the ankle, bleach-whitened teeth and perfectly painted matte-red lips which contrasted sharply with her jet-black, shiny hair, pulled tight in a chignon at the nape of her long neck.

An oriental version of Snow White, Marsha thought; it was easy to picture her pirouetting on a stage in Broadway in a modern version of the fairytale. The image helped to distract her for a few seconds, until the landing wheels engaged. The all-too familiar jolt as the plane hit the runway and then appeared to gather momentum sent a shock through her body. It never failed to alarm her that once on solid ground planes seemed to accelerate; nor did it ever prevent her from gripping the nearest solid object with such force as to turn her knuckles white. Of course she understood the science – speed being relative etc. etc., but knowledge in this case refused to turn to reason in her mind.

She had travelled light, the trip being a mere four day event and so, not having to reclaim any checked baggage, she was out of the airport with relative speed and into a shiny, black cab en-route to the hotel.

First impressions were favourable. Okay, so theoretically she'd only been in Tokyo for thirty five minutes but she was so far impressed by the business-like air of efficiency and self awareness of its people as well as the way in which everything from the floors and glass doors of the airport, to the lobby of her hotel, shone immaculately. She would take a shower, call room-service for a light snack and then hopefully get some sleep – if she was not too jet-lagged to do so.

March 10th 2011, 6:30a.m.

Neatly dressed in a fitting, grey trouser suit, Marsha rang down to reception to arrange a cab to take her to the plant at Fukushima, some one hundred and forty miles north. The three hour long journey began inland, before the highway route became more coastal. Marsha enjoyed frequent views of the sea to her right as well as the sheer rise of the mountains on her left. Nearing the vicinity of the nuclear plant, she observed that the whole area was almost totally industrial.

She finally arrived close to 10:00a.m. The cab had been cool, thanks to the air con, but on stepping outside, the humidity hit. It was different to the heat back home; that was far drier. Despite the proximity to the sea, little in the way of a breeze was to be had.

The receptionist telephoned to announce Marsha's arrival before handing her a visitor's badge. 'Will you please complete the visitor's register? Thank you,' recited the clerk in a polite but automaton voice. Marsha proceeded to fill out her details as requested.

Raising her head from the log she turned to see a rather short, slim and immaculately suited gentleman, whom she presumed to be around his mid-fifties, standing close behind her. He held out his hand and smiled.

'Hiroto Nakamura, safety manager of the nuclear fuel cycle. You are most welcome. I have looked forward to your visit and your help in our decision to upgrade our technology.'

His handshake was of the firm, two-handed kind, and his smile was warm and genuine. His English was grammatically flawless. Marsha thought his accent to be primarily North American, or perhaps Canadian, with just a trace of Japanese. Having only mailed him in order to arrange the details of the visit, Marsha had not quite known what to expect.

'Marsha Cole, pleased to meet you,' she smiled. 'Would it be possible to leave my hand luggage at reception until the end of the day?'

'But of course!' He turned to the receptionist. 'Ruka, can

you store Ms Cole's luggage securely until later please.'

He turned back to her. 'Let's get safety procedures out of the way then I can take you on a general tour of the plant so that you may familiarize yourself with the layout before we discuss any specifics.'

Marsha noted that when he smiled he did so with his whole face, not just his eyes or mouth. She was already warming to him which was somewhat out of character for her. Usually she took her time before forming a judgement, preferring to quietly observe a new acquaintance in a variety of contexts, including studying their interactions with those both above and below in the hierarchy of the working establishment. Why she did this she was not certain, though she imagined if a psychiatrist were to analyse her reasons he might declare it as having something to do with the social insecurity of her working class but highly aspirational upbringing.

The layout of the plant was fascinating. Though now considered to be relatively old she was still able to detect many modern features. As with most nuclear power plants, its attributes, such as the re-cycled seawater pumps, were determined by its location right on the edge of the coastal waters. There were so many details of the plant which contrasted with the plant back home in Arizona, purely due to the geography of the place. The Palo Verde Plant in Arizona, where she was head of safety, was the only nuclear plant in the world which was not located near a large body of water.

She and Hiroto had much to discuss on the tour. Hiroto explained that he had recently been given responsibility for updating aspects of their safety provision. He was eager to learn from Marsha's particular expertise as she was fast becoming world renowned in nuclear power safety. She soon relaxed into the visit and the general camaraderie between them became more and more informal. This was her first visit to Japan and, not one for being outside of her comfort zone, she felt safe for the first time since her arrival.

Over lunch Marsha and Hiroto shared a small table in the plant's canteen overlooking the sea. Given the views Marsha could almost imagine she was on holiday. She leaned back in her chair and relaxed a little.

'I hope you don't mind me saying, but your accent sounds American – or is it Canadian?'

'Yes, Canadian. My parents emigrated to Canada in 1968 when I was eleven years of age. My father was well educated and wanted his children to see the world. Canada was expanding in many areas of industry at the time and looking to recruit educated, English speakers from overseas. My father was offered a job as a manager in a pesticides plant. Growing up in Canada as part of a minority group however was pretty tough, especially at the age I was.'

He paused in reflection and Marsha saw his face turn pensive. 'You know, sometimes parents think that what they do for their kids is for the best, but unfortunately they don't always get it right do they?'

'I have to agree,' Marsha replied. 'You know, when you have a good career and financial success, you feel somewhat guilty about criticising the actions of your parents, but what they think is best for you does not necessarily make you happy in the long run. My dad worked twelve hour shifts in a factory, and my mom took three part time jobs in the service industry to provide my brother and I with a good education. They saved hard for us to be able to go to university. They thought they were doing what was best for us.'

She gazed out of the window to the waters beyond and sighed. 'Don't get me wrong, I'm not ungrateful; it's just that when I go back home to visit and bump into people

I was at school with, who were low academic achievers, they seem so content with their simple life. I can't help but ask myself if the struggle was worth it. It was a struggle you know – I mean on behalf of my parents. But also, like you, I know how it feels to be a minority. Even with the financial help my scholarship provided I was all too aware that I didn't really fit in Berkeley. My peers were so wealthy and spoiled; I mean even as students they all had good cars and the latest designer fashion and gadgets.'

He nodded knowingly. 'But as you grow older you re-assess what is important in life don't you? With my own children I aimed to raise them with good values and an appreciation of the joy of nature, whilst at the same time allowing them to make their own choices along the way. I hope I've achieved this, but as parents I suppose we can never be certain. I think our children tell us what they think we want to hear rather than how they actually feel, at least they do so once they have grown past the teenage years,' Hiroto grinned.

Marsha noticed that he glanced briefly at her left hand. She decided to help him out by providing a little more personal information. 'You know, I'm thirty two this year and neither married nor in a serious relationship. I don't even know if marriage and kids is what I want. I've been so focussed on my career that my personal life has been pretty non-existent.'

All the time she was speaking, she was aware of how unlike her it was to be so open with a relative stranger. She didn't know if it was jet-lag, homesickness or if it was just his manner that prompted so much honesty from her. Or perhaps it was just that lately she had begun to do some soul-searching and it was comforting to finally voice it. She had, of late, been increasingly aware of a growing sense of dissatisfaction, a feeling that she was reaching some pivotal point in her life.

She thought she'd best lighten the mood. 'You know, the only male I've ever really been in love with was a mustang,' she laughed. 'As a kid there was a rescue sanctuary for horses near home, and on weekends and holidays I would volunteer my services. I had so many happy times around those horses. Even with the sad cases – horses which had been mistreated and neglected, the sense of fulfilment I got from seeing them regain their strength and confidence around folk was so rewarding.'

Hiroto laughed. 'You know, the only advice I can offer you is that every once in a while you should pause and take a moment to listen to your heart instead of your head. Sometimes it knows us better than we know ourselves. We scientists spend far too much time on data and logical thought and not enough time on the more important aspects of life.' He paused. 'Anyway, I sound like an old man but I'm really not that old yet!'

They both laughed. 'Would you like to look at the details of the cooling system this afternoon? We can call it a day early if you wish and focus on potential updates tomorrow. I'm sure you must be tired after your long journey. You haven't even had chance to register at your hotel here at Fukushima.'

Marsha wondered if the exhaustion was beginning to manifest itself physically. She'd tried her best to conceal the dark under-eye shadows with make-up, but with the humidity, she'd needed to dab at her face several times throughout the morning. She wondered if she now resembled something like a lemur.

'That would be just great. I'm sure if I can get a good rest tonight I'll be in a better state of mind and body tomorrow. I'm embarrassed to say that I'm not the best traveller.' She felt the need to apologize for her weariness. She was enthusiastic about the visit. It was just that now that she had actually sat down and begun to relax, exhaustion seemed to overwhelm her.

'My home is fifteen miles or so from here, higher up in the mountains. I never make my home too close to work.' Hiroto explained. 'I think one needs a break from one's work. If one's home and work surroundings contrast, then one's mind can more easily make a separation. I will grant you time tonight to catch up on your sleep, but tomorrow I insist that you come to my house for dinner and meet my family.'

'That would be just great,' Marsha answered smiling. 'Hotels the whole world over are so impersonal aren't they? You could be anywhere. You never get to feel you really know a place unless you see it through the eyes of a local.'

'You know, I've been back in Japan for twenty years and it is only during the last three or four that it has finally begun to feel like home. Even though I lived here during what one assumes are the most formative years of one's life, and despite the feelings of isolation in Canada I had in my teens, once I met my wife and we made our own home there, I finally felt as though I belonged. When this job opportunity came up it took a lot of soul searching before I decided to take it. My wife's family are back in Canada but she didn't object to the move and our kids were so young then that it didn't really affect them. I think when I retire though, and the kids have made their own way in the world, I'd like to return and buy a place in the Rockies – at least that's the dream.'

'Sounds just wonderful! Don't leave it too late.'

March 11th 2011, 3:02 p.m.

So far the day had been a real success. Donned in anti-radiation suits and having completed an inspection of Reactor 2's building, Marsha and Hiroto had returned to the plant's main control room and were comparing the efficiency of Fukushima's current cooling system with the possible modifications on offer when Marsha felt the first tremor.

For the briefest of moments she assumed it was an imbalance in her ears due to the long flight. Marsha looked up from the monitor, in the hope of steadying her vision, but instead found herself being violently swayed on her stool. A glance towards Hiroto told her that the situation was not imagined. The whole room began to shake and Marsha was flung from her seat. Within seconds ceiling panels crashed to the floor, office chairs became animated and objects were hurled round the room as though by some invisible dervish hell bent on destruction.

The previous day's safety formality had taken her through the usual drills with which she was well familiar and had also included an earthquake drill. What it had not prepared her for however, was her basic, instinctual response. She attempted to steady her legs and ground herself to the spot where she half stood and half crouched, mouth agape and face ashen.

Suddenly a hand grasped hers tightly and she was pulled a few yards to take shelter under a solid desk. Hiroto tried to calm her. For him this was not an altogether new experience, for since his return to Japan he had witnessed several tremors. 'It's okay. Try to stay calm. It'll be over soon,' he said, his mouth twitching at the corners. Marsha grasped his hand tightly. She was unembarrassed. For the moment at least, she had no intention of letting go.

From beneath the desk she could see other employees who had also been working in the control room now crouched beneath similar pieces of furniture. No-one appeared particularly anxious, even though the building continued to shake. Eyes open and staring ahead she began to pray silently and to no-one in particular, as she had no belief in any deity. 'Strange that,' she thought. 'Who am I begging to make it stop? Why does one do that in an emergency even when one doesn't believe?'

But the swaying and crashing did not end. If anything it became more violent. No-one in the room spoke, though now and then, a few more-anxious employees uttered small cries.

She adjusted her position under the desk slightly to find that she was now able to see out of a window to the car park. It was the strangest sight! Cars bounced up and down in the lot, as though pressed upon by some enormous, invisible hand. Marsha was aware of her heart racing and a clammy sweat began to trickle a path inside her suit. She could not bear to look outside any longer and turned back to face Hiroto, who was also now drained of colour.

After what seemed an age, but was actually no more than a few minutes, the shaking finally subsided. 'Quick! Follow me.' Hiroto summoned Marsha out from beneath the relative safety of the desk and led her swiftly but calmly into a corridor littered with broken ceiling panels to an earthquake-proof room some hundred and fifty yards on. They were not the first to make it there. Marsha now saw that approximately twenty people were present in the room, and within moments several more appeared.

This room was approximately thirty foot square. It had no windows or furniture, other than a computer, which sat atop a sturdy looking desk screwed firmly to the floor. The ceiling was lit by a row of strip lights which were built in flush. They emitted a stark, white light, which reminded her of a recent visit to the dentist during which she had undergone a root canal. Her head started to ache in sympathy. She gazed around the room, still in shock. Taking a few deep breaths, in an attempt to slow her heart rate, she stared about her. Everyone was speaking in anxious tones, but the rapid, Japanese dialogue rendered the situation very disorientating. She felt as though she were dreaming.

'Please excuse me,' Hiroto spoke to her calmly now, bringing her thoughts back to the present as would a hypnotist. 'There are several senior staff present. I must speak with them. They are deciding on the best response to the earthquake. Try to stay calm. There may be smaller aftershocks but you will be safe here. I will return to you in just a minute.'

As Hiroto left to join the others, Marsha suddenly felt as though her legs might buckle. She managed two or three strides, before slumping to the floor, where she leaned against comfort of the cool, solid wall.

Approximately five minutes later Marsha heard several mobiles ringing, ensued by hasty discussions. Hiroto returned and sat on the floor beside her. 'Units one to three have gone into automatic shut-down, and units four to six are currently out of operation for maintenance, so there's no need to worry – the situation will almost certainly resume to normal soon.' He attempted a smile but Marsha read the concern in his eyes. She tried to smile back. Although no-one else in the room was seated she remained on the floor, still visibly shaken. She was sure that given that she was a visitor, who would, as such, be unfamiliar with such a situation, her lack of etiquette would be forgiven, even in a country world renowned for its protocol.

'There's just one potential problem at the moment,' Hiroto continued. 'The external power supplies appear to have been lost. She must have been powerful! It's never happened before. We're just waiting for confirmation that the emergency diesel generators in the basements have kicked in, though I'm sure they will have.'

'I'm sorry I'm not much use at the moment Hiroto. I think I'm in shock. Head of Safety and I go into meltdown!'

'Ah, it's understandable,' he said, patting her hand kindly. 'Until you've lived through an earthquake you haven't a clue as to how you will react. Don't worry.'

'But you'd think coming from an earthquake belt myself I'd be used to it. We've had many small quakes back home, but I've never felt one as powerful as that.'

Moments later an important looking gentleman, who Marsha noted was not wearing an anti-radiation suit, approached and spoke to Hiroto. A senior colleague, Marsha assumed from his clothing and the rapport between them. However, she was finding the placement of rank more difficult in Japan, as all the people she had met so far seemed very courteous. She studied Hiroto's face closely as they talked, in order to glean possible clues as to the slant of the conversation. It was good news.

'It's okay. We have confirmation that no serious damage has been done to the reactors. Cooling has been maintained and the aftershocks have subsided – at least for the present. We'll return to the control room and see the situation for ourselves now.'

A wave of relief flooded over Marsha. The knot in her stomach loosened and her breathing eased.

A glimpse into the control room confirmed that it had been evacuated by all. It appeared as though burgled. Office contents were scattered around the room and everything was pretty torn up. Hiroto switched the computer on to check for himself that the diesel generators had kicked in.

Just as he did so the first huge wave hit.

Marsha saw it first. Gazing out of the window, she could not believe her eyes. She barely had time to call Hiroto's name before the immense wall of water hit. The glass window panes shattered on contact. Within a split second she found herself knocked off her feet and struggling to find ground in a pool of swirling sea water, surrounded by debris. But it was the noise which was most terrifying. Her ears were filled with a cacophony of sounds which metabolised into one tumultuous, pitch of rage and fear. She gasped for breath as her head went under for the umpteenth time. For a moment she felt a strange sense of peace. At least here, under the water, the sound was muted. Then instinct kicked in and she fought to re-emerge. She was aware that every time she came up the water level had risen, and all this had taken but a few seconds.

'Hiroto!' she managed to scream. But he did not reply.

Suddenly all power was lost. Not only was she barely keeping her head afloat but now she was also plunged into almost total darkness. She began to shiver. She screamed his name again. 'Hiroto! Where are you?'

'Marsha, is that you? I'm over here. Hold tight, I'll try to make my way over. Keep calling so I know which direction to swim.'

She did as she was asked, though it was difficult, as the water was so volatile. It continued to swirl and gush and she was constantly hit by indistinguishable objects. Raising her arm above the level of the water she was just about able to touch what remained of the ceiling. She knew without doubt, that if the water level rose much higher, they would drown. The absence of light made it so much worse.

Just then she heard a gasp which was not her own and felt Hiroto's hand reach out to her. They clung to each other in the chaos, both too exhausted to speak. It was enough of a struggle just to remain in contact with one another.

Seconds passed and Marsha became aware that the flow of the water had calmed somewhat. Once again she reached up her arm towards the ceiling. 'It's stopped rising. Thank God! In fact, it seems a little lower.'

'There's nothing we can do,' Hiroto replied. 'We just need to try and hang on and hope that soon the water level will fall. The sea should pull back soon. If it does we'll try to get out of this room and into a higher part of the building in case there's a second wave. Are you hurt?'

'I don't think so, but I'm so cold I feel pretty numb.

How about you?'

'Same here, though I think I have a gash on my head judging by the way it's pounding. I'm okay though. My God I can't believe it! The earthquake must have caused a tsunami. If it's submerged the pumps for the condenser circuits in the basement the situation could be dire. There's more than our own lives at stake here Marsha.'

Marsha began to tremble so violently that even her teeth chattered. She had never before known such fear and desperation. It was too much to take in.

Just then something tugged violently at her right leg. It was trying to pull her under the water. The top of her head submerged. Hiroto had felt it too and pulled hard at the arm he had been gripping. She kicked as hard as she could and felt herself free. Re-emerging she spluttered, gasping for breath.

'What happened?' Hiroto yelled.

'I don't know! I think my leg must have snagged on some debris below. It felt as if it was pulling me down.'

They tread water rhythmically, in an attempt to stay afloat.

'It's gone really quiet,' Marsha whispered. 'So eerie!'

They both felt it at the same time. This time there was no doubt. Despite the almost total blackout, they knew they were being deliberately pulled below the surface of the water. This was no debris! Whatever it was that seemed hell bent on their demise was alive.

Marsha barely managed to fill her lungs with air before once again being violently hauled beneath the surface. She was aware that she no longer held contact with Hiroto but could not tell whether or not he remained close by. She only knew that this *thing* held her in what she assumed were its jaws and it had no intention this time of letting go.

Instinct kicked in and she fought as hard as she could to re-surface. Arms flailing she punched blindly, repeatedly

140

jerking her torso back and fore. She felt a bump to her head as it made contact with another, which she assumed was Hiroto's. From hip level to ankles her legs were imprisoned in a vice-like grip. This creature was now her jailor. She was not going to escape.

She felt her lungs deflate. She knew she was going to die. A sudden feeling of calm resignation filled her mind and her body went limp. The struggle was over.

Just as her eyes closed, a powerful surge of water freed her body and she was thrust upwards and forwards in the dark. Her head broke the surface and she seized a breath. The water was being sucked back out now, almost as violently as it had arrived. She opened her eyes and noticed that there was suddenly more light. Her limp body bounced off the wall of the room. The water level was window height. She reached out a hand and clung on to the glassless frame in an attempt to prevent her body from being sucked out of the gap and into the vast sea of debris beyond. A jagged shard of glass buried itself deep in her palm, yet for a moment there was no pain. 'Hiroto!' She tried to scream, but her voice sounded pathetically small in the once again deafening roar of the sea.

She had given up hope. She did not expect him to reply, nor did she expect to live to tell this tale. She was not even certain that she was alive. Maybe this was it. Perhaps she was being taken somewhere else. Maybe your journey to wherever it was you went after life depended on the cause of your death. The wave had come in, and with it something else, and now it was trying to take her back out. Yet the little logic that remained failed to make sense of this. She knew that at the end of this life there was nothing – just eternal blackness.

It was shocking to suddenly hear her own name being called and by a familiar voice. Nudged back to reality she called his name again. 'Hiroto?'

He emerged from under the water, near to where she still grasped the window, spitting and retching as he did so.

'What just happened?' she asked.

'The sea has retreated. What held us prisoner? I was certain that it would kill us. It felt so powerful! We didn't imagine it did we?'

'No Hiroto. I felt it too. It was hell bent on taking us with it back to wherever it had come from. Even though I could see nothing, I could sense its calm determination. It must have come in with the wave. Could it have been a huge fish – a shark or something?'

'Possibly, but I have never heard of anything so big. I mean it held us both in its jaws. Whatever it was it has probably found its way back out to sea. Look Marsha – the water level has subsided to half what it was and there is more daylight. Look–' Hiroto pointed to another part of the room. 'The door is off its hinges. We should be able to swim out and get to a higher room. It's likely that a second wave will hit soon and I don't want to be here when that happens. I don't think we'd have any chance of surviving another wave, in fact, I can't believe we're alive!'

With what little strength remained, they swam towards the gap in the wall and out into the corridor. It was darker here, the only light coming from the room which they had left behind. 'Hold on to my leg. I know the way to the stairs.'

The light once again grew dimmer and dimmer as they made painful, slow progress along the corridor. Every time something bumped into Marsha she was instantly reminded of the *thing* that had pulled her under. She tried to resist kicking out when this happened, as she knew it would make it even more difficult for Hiroto who was already struggling to gain any distance with her holding onto him. She felt a sudden jolt and they came to an abrupt halt. They clung to each other.

'We've reached the stairs,' he panted. 'Hold out your left arm and you will feel them. Do you think you have enough strength to pull yourself out of the water?'

Marsha used the last of her strength to heave her battered body upwards. Almost deliriously she managed to lift her feet, one after another, until she could sense that she was now completely on dry land. She felt about to collapse with exhaustion.

'Come on! We're not safe yet. We must climb higher. There's another two levels above. Take my arm and I'll help you.'

Marsha's chest heaved with each step. Her lungs seared hot with the effort. Despite the dehydration her mouth pumped with saliva, and her head felt as if it would burst.

Finally they reached the top. The first door relented easily to Hiroto's push. She felt her way into the room, as would a blind person, and closed the door behind them. A little light shone from the one small window at the far end of the room. The room - which had obviously been a small office - was now desecrated by quake damage. Nevertheless it felt like heaven. It was dry and relatively warm.

They stumbled over to the small window and looked out. The sight that met them was hard to believe. The window overlooked the front of the building. The main road outside no longer existed. Vehicles, all kinds of debris, including houses and other buildings had been swept away by the wave and then piteously dumped wherever the sea had abandoned them. The scene was one of utter devastation; no sign of life, neither human nor animal, yet despite the disorder there seemed a strange sense of calm, as if the world had been put into an oversize washing machine which had now completed its cycle and was just waiting to be unloaded.

'We'll have to wait it out here. We should know within

minutes if further waves are coming. If not we'll try to get out and see what we can do to help,' Hiroto said.

They sat on the floor in silence for a few moments. 'Do you really believe that whatever pulled us under retreated with the wave?' Marsha asked.

'I'm pretty certain it would have done. I mean, there was no sign of it in the control room afterwards was there? Anyway, even if it didn't leave and is still down there somewhere, at least we can be certain that it was brought in by the wave so it must be aquatic. There is no way it could climb up here. If there is a second wave it wouldn't be as high as the first - they never are - so the water level would likely be lower not higher.'

'That's some comfort at least,' Marsha replied, leaning her head on his shoulder, desperate for fellow comfort. 'It was terrifying wasn't it? I've never before felt so powerless. The water was one thing, but at least once I knew it had reached its highest level, I also realized that it was just down to our own ability to stay afloat. I didn't factor in a second demon!'

They remained on the floor, examining their injuries. The cut to Marsha's hand was pretty bad. Now that she was out of the water it bled profusely. Amongst the debris Hiroto found a jacket. Managing to tear off a strip from the sleeve, he made a tourniquet to bind her wound.

The bump to his own head produced little blood, but a lump the size of an egg stood proudly.

Marsha was aware of quite severe pain around the circumference of her hips. With his help, she unzipped the soaking anti-radiation suit and pulled it down. A band of angry, purpling bruises greeted her. 'This is where it grabbed me,' she said. 'See if you have similar marks.'

Slightly higher, towards the waist area, Hiroto wore a similar bruise. Marsha's left hip and Hiroto's right side though were bruise free, which confirmed that whatever it was had encircled them as one.

She estimated that it must have been close to ten minutes since the first wave had retreated. From the small window, they watched the sea intently. It appeared almost benign, innocent. Suddenly, on the far horizon, they sighted the second wave.

Watching it move closer and closer was the most surreal experience imaginable. It was an enormous, moving grey wall, its ferocity immense! When the first wave had struck, neither of them had been aware of its approach until it was almost upon them. This was different. Even though Hiroto had assured her that it would likely be less damaging, she was never the less terrified.

Helplessly, they watched it consume the floating buildings in its path, before once again hitting the plant. The roar of the water flooding the rooms below for a second time, and the clanging of the crashing debris within the building was deafening. Even here, two floors above sea level, Marsha could sense the vibration beneath her feet. She could only hope that this particular part of the plant had been built with deep enough foundation to withstand the force. She knew this was likely given its purpose, but still she felt another wave of panic as the world outside once again completely submerged.

From this height, it appeared as though someone had built a miniature landscape and then - being dissatisfied with the creation - had chosen to swipe it all away. The strangest thing was the absence of human voices. She assumed that by now, most people who had been inside the plant or in its vicinity were either dead or remained hidden within the bowels of the earthquake-proof rooms.

'We can do nothing but sit this out,' Hiroto said. The positions of responsibility that both of them held meant there was an element of guilt behind their inaction, though without giving it voice, both knew that they really could do nothing more under present circumstances. They sat on the floor exhausted, waiting, hoping that once again the wave would soon recede.

The calamitous sounds once again gradually subsided in the rooms below as the contents settled into a floating position. Then a new sound; a recurring and rhythmic flopping which seemed to amplify by the second. She sprang to her feet. She was sure something was climbing the stairs. 'Did you hear that?'

'What?'

'Sh! Listen. I think something's climbing the stairs.'

For a moment there was silence, just the sound of the lapping sea and the occasional clang as objects hit each other on their unintended journey. Then Hiroto heard it too. He too sprang up and rushed towards the door.

'No wait!' shouted Marsha. 'What if it's the *thing* from earlier?'

'That's impossible! It can't be! It came from the sea and returned to the sea!' He had almost reached the door now. 'There's someone out there. They're probably hurt and are trying to drag themselves to safety. We must help!'

Reaching the door handle, he yanked it open. Marsha remained at the far end of the room...

'Is anyone there?' Hiroto called into the gloom.

The stench hit them first; a rotting, filthy reek of decay, so powerful that she gagged even though she was more than twenty feet away.

Hiroto was swept off his feet. His legs were pulled from beneath him and he was dragged swiftly from the doorway where he had stood just a second earlier. It happened so quickly that Marsha did not even see the thing that had attacked. All she heard was the sickening thud of

Hiroto's head as it made contact with the ground. She stood motionless. Instinct told her to remain where she was. On the other side of the doorway she was aware of a sliding, thudding sound as the *thing* dragged Hiroto down the stairs.

All her life she had experienced fear of one kind or another – she had never managed to conquer it! Fear had always controlled her. Something clicked in her head. It was as if an invisible hand had flicked a switch in the darkness. She knew Hiroto had been knocked unconscious by the fall. If she did not possess the strength to help him he would certainly be lost – if he were not already dead.

She crossed the room in a few paces and headed into the corridor. She screamed his name into the darkness, knowing that this time he would not answer. Never before had she felt such anger. It was as though all the negativity of her life so far had gathered momentum and become its own tsunami.

Marsha knew that it had taken him back down the stairs. It wanted him within its own domain, where it was master. She ran down them in the dark, with little regard for her own safety. At the bottom she plunged into the cold, swirling water and blindly splashed along the corridor through which, just minutes earlier, they had swum together; he then the strong one and she the meek follower.

Within seconds she knew she had found the right place. A cursory glance at her surroundings confirmed she was back in the main control room. She recognized the shape of the window which had damaged her hand. Her eyes scanned the dark water but saw nothing. The whole room lapped gently, innocently, womb-like.

'Hiroto!' she screamed, her anger intensified. It was a raging bull, injured by the matador. She stood still, waist deep in the murk. From the far left corner of the room there came a sound. It was small, a mere ripple, but nevertheless distinguishable from the lapping. Without hesitation she plunged into the water, aiming for the place where she knew it held him. She was aware of the likelihood of the outcome for them both, but her own survival instinct was suddenly snuffed-out. All she felt was rage; pure, uncontaminated resentment towards this *thing* which, not being satisfied with the deaths caused by the water, was greedy enough to desire yet another. She knew it was waiting patiently for the water to retreat; then it would take Hiroto with it, back to the sea and maybe beyond, back to wherever it had come from.

Filling her lungs with air, she dived. It was impossible to see, but she could feel. She was in control. She released the precious air from her lungs only gradually, all the time feeling about with both hands. No panic; instead she was possessed by a calm she had never before experienced.

Suddenly her left hand brushed against hair. She grabbed and held on tight. Yes, it was his head. This would be her one and only chance. She knew he might already be lost. Unless his head had been kept above water whilst the *thing* carried him, he would not have survived, but still she refused to give up. If the *thing* tried to grab her too, it would firstly have to release Hiroto.

Reaching forward to where she guessed his shoulders would be, she latched on to the flesh beneath the slippery suit and held tight. With a firm grip, she pulled his limp body towards her but felt him held firm at the feet. Whatever grasped him at the other end did not even need to pull. It just waited, patiently, as though it knew her cause was lost. Twice more she pulled but it was useless. She knew that she would either have to return to the surface for air or die with him.

She was just about to let go when she felt it for the second time. The pull of the sea was an Olympic tug of war. The thing which held Hiroto was powerful, but it was nothing compared to the might of the sea. Without even realizing it she clung on to Hiroto's shoulders, as gravity sucked them once again towards the distant light...

March 11th 2012

Marsha watched from the window in eager anticipation as the tiny two-person plane hit the short runway in the hills of South Dakota. A smile of exhilaration lit her tanned face as it decelerated to a stop.

Thanking the pilot, she jumped down and headed straight for the Jeep that would take her to the mustang rescue sanctuary. Her tangled hair blew wildly in the wind as she bent down to re-tie the laces of her sturdy walking boots.

Installed in the cosiness of her tent, she began to write. The absence of internet and mobile connection here meant she would have to do things the old-fashioned way.

She couldn't believe that it had been a whole year; but what a year! She really must write to him today and tell him her news...

Dearest Hiroto,

How are you? I hope you are making good progress along your own path of enlightenment.

Can you believe that a whole year has passed by? How is that cabin in the woods coming along? Is it as beautiful as you imagined in the Rockies? I so look forward to visiting both you and Jaydeen in the fall. I have so much to tell you! I don't know where to start, so I'll begin by letting you know just how very happy I am ...

Charity

(A Modern-day Christmas Carol)

You better watch out,
You better not cry,
You better not pout,
I'm telling you why...
Satan Claws is coming to town!

Acol's Advertising Agency, Hove, November 2012
'Gotta be in the boardroom at 8:00a.m. sharp Troy. New boss has called a meeting.'

'Yeah, I heard,' Troy drawled. 'James messaged me last night.'

Dan clapped his hands annoyingly close to Troy's hungover ears. 'Come on then, get a move on! Don't wanna be late! Heard she's a stickler for time keeping.'

'Yeah yeah – stickler for a lot of things I hear. Supposed to be a right bitch!'

'True mate, but we mustn't moan. At least it's a chance to keep this place going. We came so close to going bust. I honestly thought I'd be out of a job by Christmas, so I don't really care what she's like as long as she keeps us afloat! The talk is that she saved her last place from going down the swanny, so in my opinion she's worth a shot.'

'S'ppose so,' Troy agreed grudgingly. 'Have to pay the rent don't we? Though to be honest with you Dan, I'm already applying for jobs elsewhere. I mean, just 'cos she saved one place from going bust, doesn't necessarily mean she can do it again.'

*

151

'Morning ladies and gentleman.' Alison Jackman breezed confidently into the boardroom: figure-hugging Chanel skirt suit, tanned bare legs and killer heels. The greeting was amiable enough, though neither a hint of a smile nor a flicker of warmth accompanied the gesture. With eagle eyes she scanned the row of staff who had all stood to attention as she entered. An immaculately French-polished finger indicated that they could be seated, before she embarked on her inauguration speech.

'Okay– I'm not going to beat about the bush. For those of you to whom I have not yet been introduced, my name is Alison Jackman. I'm not going to pretend to be something I'm not. I prefer to be honest with you all from day one; either you're in this for the long-haul or you can leave right now.'

She paused, as if to provide a chance for those unconvinced to take their leave. When no-one moved she continued. 'This business is on its knees. I won't share the exact figures with you all here and now – I'll reserve that little pleasure for the finance committee later, but believe me when I say that we're in the red by a substantial amount and without drastic action you'll all be out of work in the new year.'

She paused again and scanned the length of the boardroom only to be met with two rows of lowered eyes. 'So, we all have to work hard and be prepared to make what some of you might consider pretty tough decisions if this place is to have any hope of rising from the proverbial ashes.'

She flashed a flicker of a tooth-whitened smirk in the direction of Rory McCinnes, financial director. 'I'm sure that some of you will already have been informed that my methods can be pretty ruthless, but times are tough. As I've said, it's fight or flight I'm afraid. If anyone feels inclined to hand in their resignation after reading the new job description, which has been prepared for each and every one of you, then please feel free to do so.' Again she scanned the room, sizing up each and every one of them before continuing in an acidic tone, 'There's plenty more fish in the sea as they say.' This last sentence, delivered with a contemptuous sniff, caused Troy's hackles to rise.

The room remained silent. All assembled fixed their gaze on any inanimate object which just so happened to be within their line of vision.

*

'Fucking recession!' Troy muttered to Dan under his breath, when he considered they were out of earshot of the boardroom. He pitied the members of the finance committee who remained seated in the throes of what could only be termed *a dressing-down*. Through the glass, he observed their pale faces. 'They look as if they've shit themselves! Got us by the balls hasn't she? Not that easy to find a job these days, especially if you've come from a failed business!'

During morning break, the staffroom was eerily empty. Many of the twenty seven employees were too afraid of getting pulled into a derogatory conversation about the new boss by a more rebellious member of staff and so had simply skipped break altogether. Other staff members had slipped away in search of a private space in which they could peruse the new job description which had been handed to them at the end of the meeting.

Help for the Homeless Shelter, Hove 8th December 2012

Joe Prenderson, manager of the charitable establishment, was aghast at the letter he had just received. 'Why, the stingy low-down bastards!' he muttered aloud, despite the fact that no-one else was present. Leaping from his seat, he went in search of Brenda Collins, his receptionist, cook and general life-saver, who was just about to pour a cup of tea in the tiny soup kitchen at the back of the building. She registered the look of shock on his face even before he spoke.

'What's the matter Joe? Sit down – you look as if you're about to pass out!'

Beads of clammy sweat glistened on his top lip. Waving the sheet of white paper in front of her he ranted, 'Of all the mean, low-down stunts to pull Brend, this one takes the biscuit!' Slumping down unsteadily on the wobbly kitchen stool, he held his head in both hands.

'What's happened? For Christ's sake, tell me!'

Joe stabbed at the sheet of paper with a fat, pink digit. 'Fifteen years they've donated to the Christmas fund. Fifteen years without a miss and now they've pulled the rug from under our feet!'

'What you talking about Joe? You're not making any sense!' Brenda was trembling, though she'd still made no sense of Joe's news. She simply gleaned from the look on his face that it was not good.

Joe's next words were accompanied by a sobbing sigh. 'We've had a letter Brend – look.' With a trembling hand, he passed over the offensive document. 'It's from Acol's Agency. You know the grand they give us every year to fund the Christmas dinner? Well they've gone and pulled out on us two weeks before Christmas!' He paused, watching her face turn ashen as she devoured the contents of the unsavoury letter. 'You know, I thought it was fishy! We usually receive the cheque from them by the end of November at the latest, in plenty of time for us to do the order, but I didn't like to give them a ring – seemed a bit cheeky like. I can't believe they've left it so late to tell us. That's gutless that is! We haven't even got time to whip-up a fund-raise now!' He emitted a desperate groan. 'What we gonna do Brend?'

Brenda finished reading the letter and began to cry. 'Oh my God Joe! What we gonna do? Without their donation there will *be* no Christmas dinner! They must know we count on it – I can't believe they've done this!' She plonked herself down on the stool opposite his before her legs gave way. 'Surely they must realize how desperate this place is at Christmas! I mean we've always shown our gratitude haven't we Joe?We've never taken it for granted! What the hell we gonna do?'

Canteen, Help for the Homeless – same day

Joe and Brenda fed the regulars as usual, attempting to put on a brave face as they did so. It was minus three outside and many of them had come in frozen to the bone. They couldn't bear to give them the bad news – at least not until they'd been fed and watered. Many of the men and women now gathered in the little canteen had been coming to the shelter for several years. Others were more transient, but Joe and Brenda still recognised every face in front of them. Christmas was always the most difficult time of year and the regulars looked forward to the feast and entertainment provided by the shelter.

When they had finished eating, and were gathered in their usual little cliques, Joe spoke up. 'Excuse me guys... I need a word.' The room fell silent. He cleared his throat and began shakily. 'I'm afraid we've had some bad news today.' All eyes fixed on him. 'Many of you know that our funding comes purely from charity. Well, the advertising agency down the road has always given us the money for the Christmas bash, but today I received a letter from their new Chief Executive, a certain Ms Alison Jackman, stating that they were pulling the funds this year.' He resisted eye contact as he delivered the news.

For several moments the room was silent, then Charlie Waters, an old veteran of the establishment, piped up.

'What you saying Joe? There'll *be* no Christmas dinner this year?'

Joe visibly flinched. 'Doesn't look like it Charlie. Me and Brend are in shock. We can't believe they've left it 'til now to tell us. We only found out this morning and at the moment we're stuck as to what to do!'

Now everyone spoke at the same time. The room erupted into a cacophony of dismay.

'You got any paper I can borrow Joe?' Charlie asked, when things had calmed down a bit. 'I'm not gonna let them get away with this! The least I can do is write a letter explaining how we all feel. None of us want to beg; we all wish we didn't have to rely on charity, but the mean sods shouldn't be allowed to get away with this, especially as they're so late in telling you.'

Charlie shuffled off behind Joe towards the office, to fetch pen and paper.

'If you want any help with that letter Charlie let me know,' Joe offered respectfully. Seeing the despondency in Charlie's cataract-clouded eyes caused his heart to flip.

'No thanks. I'll write it meself if you don't mind Joe. I'm not the best speller in the world, but I think I can make meself understood. This way I can say exactly what I think.'

'Course Charlie; it might be better coming from you. After all, you're the poor buggers whose Christmas will be ruined.'

Retreating to an empty corner of the canteen, Charlie sat down and began to pen the letter.

Christmas Eve 2012, Alison Jackman's house, Brighton

At precisely 11:45p.m., Alison turned the key and entered the capacious hallway of her Victorian semi. Whisking the security chain across, she slipped out of her pale-grey MaxMara coat and slung it over the banister. Entering the living room, she flicked on the light, before kicking off her six inch high Louboutin's and padding barefoot across the plush, cream carpet.

Her frown was a thunderstorm. 'Who the *fuck* does he think he is!' she muttered under her breath, still annoyed that the little tosser Dan had actually had the audacity to hit on her. Okay, so he *had* knocked back a good few drinks - that much was obvious - but that didn't give him the right to lay a finger on her. How fucking dare he? She shuddered as she recalled the warmth of his fingers tracing the length of her spine. She had turned around abruptly only to come face to face with – him! A cloud of bourbon-laced breath had wafted at her as he'd slurred, 'You gonna be lonely tonight darling?'

She had wanted to slap his face but knew it would only have caused a scene in the bar where they were all gathered for a few Christmas drinks. She understood only too well that several of those present would have thoroughly enjoyed witnessing her lashing out, but she wasn't going to grant them that pleasure!

They'd worked until 7:00p.m., as usual. She'd had no intention of letting them out early just because it was bloody Christmas Eve – not with the place in the appalling mess it was. Why should she? No – they'd have to prove themselves worthy before she'd be prepared to slacken the reins. Too bloody soft the old boss had been – that was why the business was in the state it was.

Anyway, she'd grudgingly gone along to the bar, just to show her face, intending to be home by nine thirty, but one G&T had led to another and before she'd known it, it had gone eleven. Then that slime ball had actually touched her up and ruined her evening! 'I'll have him out by March!' she promised herself through gritted teeth.

Alison slumped down on her beige, leather sofa for a few seconds then quickly shot up and stumbled to the bathroom. Her head spun. Was it simply because she had got up too quickly or was it the five G&T's she had necked?

She quickly stripped, leaving her black dress strewn on the floor, and jumped into the shower, enjoying the flow of hot water caressing her body. Slipping into a pair of midnight-blue silk pyjamas, she padded barefoot back to the living room. Lighting some exotic candles on top of the mantelpiece, she poured herself another G&T and flopped back down on the sofa.

The room seemed eerily quiet so, locating the remote for the Bluetooth, she scrolled through her play list before selecting Amy Winehouse. No fucking Christmas music for her – what a load of trite nonsense that was!

Feet up, she tried to focus on the lyrics in an attempt to divert her thoughts. However, the task of having to visit her mother in the dementia home the following morning refused to shift. Could I get away with ringing instead, she wondered? Perhaps I could make an excuse and say I have flu. Grudgingly she admitted that she couldn't very well do that as she'd arranged to go straight from there to her sister and brother in law's for lunch. When they would visit Mum later the subject of her being at theirs would be bound to arise.

Perhaps I'll cancel that as well she decided; after all, a traditional family Christmas lunch did little to motivate her. Truth be told she'd rather spend the day on her own, eating and drinking what she wanted and watching whatever she chose on t.v. than have to endure someone else's inane choice – or worse still, some shitty party game! Perhaps she would cancel. She'd make her mind up in the morning.

Closing her eyes, she inhaled the subtle scent of midnight jasmine...

The chorus of *Back to Black* played soothingly,

enchantingly. She sung along, glass in hand, slurring a little.

A rustle from the fireplace made her bolt upright.

Nothing.

Probably the wind loosening some soot. The track had switched to *I'm No Good*. Eyes closed, she grinned, revelling in the lyrics' message, indulging herself for a few moments in the memory of Robin, the sycophantic leech who was now well and truly her ex.

Without warning, an intense heat suddenly engulfed her. She sensed the presence in the room even before she opened her eyes. It took less than half a second for her half-drunk brain to register the demonic, red-clad being looming over her.

It gazed at her greedily - a ruthless grin splitting its face from ear to ear - before its claws tore into her flesh.

No time to fight back! Her torso ripped from navel to breast bone in one fell swoop. Midnight silk instantly soaked crimson and dripped onto the beige leather. Not even time to scream...

Christmas Day, 4:00pm, 2012

After Alison had failed to turn up for lunch as arranged, and countless attempts to reach her mobile had gone unanswered, her sister had phoned the police. She met them at the front door but had no key – Alison never trusted anyone enough to leave a spare.

Having broken down the door, the two officers crossed the hall and entered the living room, from which the sickly-sweet smell of blood was faintly traceable to an accustomed nose. There, sprawled at a contorted angle on the sofa, lay Alison's body – or at least what remained of it.

On exposed, pink ribs a bloody note lay patiently waiting...

Deeu Satan Claws,

I wood like to tell u wot has just append to owu xmas dinnur. This womun called Alissun Jackman who is the new boss of Acol Adverts in Hove has stopt the money they always send to owu homeless charity. This meens we wont av no xmas dinnur this year. We are gutted! We no you always elp uvers in need at xmas. Can you elp us Satan?

Thanks

Charlie Waters

They never did find the culprit.

Shams

Nose pressed to the window of the Boeing 777, Anwar couldn't help but smile.

'Doesn't the light hurt your eyes?' asked the elderly and rather austere gentleman on his left.

'No – not in the slightest!' Anwar replied wistfully.

His answer met with a rather disgruntled *harrumph,* followed by an exaggerated shake of a broadsheet copy of The Times, which Anwar was certain had already been digested from cover to cover. He dared a sidelong glance at the man and saw that he had angled the newspaper so that it covered the whole of his face and hence blocked out the light. Out of a sense of politeness, Anwar fleetingly considered asking his neighbour if he would prefer the blind closed, but instead decided to behave selfishly. After all, this may be his last chance for some time to bask in the glorious rays before the inevitable grey of London would engulf him. Still, he would cope. Ultimately, he considered himself so very fortunate to have been granted such a wonderful opportunity.

*

Some three weeks earlier, Anwar had received the news that he had been selected for the Professorship in Quantum Technologies at U.C.L. He had worked extremely hard over the years and had performed to his utmost during the interviews in order to secure this dream-post.

There was just one fly in the ointment – and no, it wasn't that he would miss his beloved family, it was that he would miss the sun. Anwar laughed rather too loudly at how ridiculous this sounded, even to himself, causing his flight neighbour to *harrumph* a second time.

Never mind, it was early September, so with any luck there would still be a few weeks of British Summer Time to enjoy before the days grew short and the nights long. And in any case, he would be so busy in the new post he doubted he would have time to dwell on the weather.

Was it mere coincidence, he wondered, that his choice of career path had so much to do with the study of light? Possibly – and yet as far back as he could remember he had seized every opportunity to spend time outdoors, basking in the rays. Why, even his name, Anwar meant *illuminated*. Talk about the theory of nominative determinism!

Anwar thought back to the gloomy, rain-soaked week he had spent in London July past, during which, the seemingly endless rounds of interviews and meetings for the post had taken place. He had been so entirely enthused by the physical environment and ethos of the university campus that, at least during the day, he had managed to forget the weather. And yet during those six long, lonely evenings, when he had remained cooped-up in his hotel room – well, that had been a different matter.

Anwar recalled the final and less formal of the interviews. He had considered the question *Where do you see yourself in ten years time?* rather predictable and yet, in retrospect, he supposed he could see its value. For if it were enthusiasm and vision that they sought, the question - predictable or otherwise - had provided him the opportunity to convey his passion for assisting the physicists of the future in their understanding of the potential for quantum computerization. The point of discussion had enabled him to articulate with first-hand knowledge about how he had been part of the ground-breaking team who'd been instrumental in developing quantum dot technology.

Most importantly, it had enabled him to convey to the Board the importance of being a team player. He shivered slightly. His recollection of the break-through they'd made still had the power to make his spine tingle– and now he would have the opportunity to share this knowledge with the future generation of Quantum Physicists in one of the best universities in the world. Incredible!

No, he would not allow something as insignificant as the weather to sour his chance at embarking on a new chapter in life.

Shams - Arabic for *sun*. He sighed, and for a few moments allowed his tired cinnamon-brown eyes to close. Maybe he was already suffering a little home-sickness but did not want to admit it to himself.

*

Three weeks had passed. Three whole weeks of getting to know new colleagues, and students, and the city. It had flown by in a bustling haze of activity. He had hardly had a moment to think about home, or family and certainly not the weather! But that was playing ball at present – indeed, each day so far had dawned bright and glorious and had certainly helped to motivate and energize him for the challenges ahead.

This coming week though he would need to switch his focus to finding a place to live; temporary student accommodation really wouldn't befit a faculty professor long term. He had a few viewings lined up, and Yan, who had already become a friend as well as a colleague, had volunteered to accompany him. Having lived in London for the past eight years, Yan had a far better idea of the property market than Anwar, and so, the previous Sunday, they'd trawled the net and local estate agents and had managed to whittle the viewings down to four apartments. If none proved suitable then Anwar would have to delay the house-hunt for another three weeks as he'd organized a field trip with a few, select students to a ground-breaking quantum computing company in California. He laughed.

At least there he would be almost guaranteed a further three weeks of sunshine!

*

He knew the moment he stepped inside the door of the second apartment that it was *the one*. From its fully glazed open-plan ground floor, the view of Canary Wharf was completely uninterrupted. No walls, no panelling, no doors – just ten metres of perfect panorama.

'I'll take it!' He beamed at the agent without a hint of concern for the rental figure. Yes, it would stretch his budget, but wasn't that why he worked so hard? And after all, he had no dependants to worry about. He strode over towards the seamless, sliding panel and stepped straight out onto the balcony.

'Ah!' Anwar inhaled deeply, both with relief at having so easily found the place of his dreams and the way in which the early evening saffron-sun sauntered along the Thames.

*

Eleven straight hours in the excited company of eight emerging adults, this time in economy class, and he was exhausted! Still, ascending from the plane the hot air hit him full in the face and the mirage of heat-haze on tarmac soared his spirits.

And what a trip it was! To spend time in such exuberant and assiduous company was a breath of fresh air. So much shared thinking, so many questions, so much positive debate. It quenched his thirst more than a crisp Napa Valley Chardonnay. And to witness the exuberance of his students was a joy. After all, he was forty-nine years old; they were the future – the generation who would most likely bring about the developments in quantum technology that were so essential for sustained progression in this world.

Disembarking from the plane at Heathrow however could

not have been a more different experience. A jinn-like, ominous mist enveloped the city as far as the eye could see. No wind – just a still, brittle cold that penetrated Anwar's light-weight jacket. He shivered and clenched his teeth. The terminal building was no warmer; in fact, he was grateful for the intimacy of the long passport control queue, but despite the thousands of bodies thronging the *Arrivals* hall, the wait for his luggage was uncomfortably chilly.

Somewhat cheered by a long, hot shower, Anwar threw together a snack, put on some Khaliji and reflected on the success of the field trip. The weekend stretched ahead. At least he had two days of rest before lectures were due to resume.

He awoke abruptly at 3:00a.m., soaked in perspiration, a cold, acidic sweat that usually accompanies a fever. Shivering violently he crawled out of bed and headed for the kitchen, cursing the trapped bacteria that multiply exponentially in the humidity of cabin air. Two paracetamol and a large glass of water later, he dragged himself back to bed.

Delirium - *an acutely disturbed state of mind characterized by restlessness, illusions, and incoherence.*

What a night! Anwar woke the next morning feeling as though he'd been beaten by an Ifrit. He could stomach no food but managed to sustain hydration by downing several glasses of cold water and as many paracetamol as he presumed safe. The weather was as grey and dull as his head. He lay on the sofa, huddled in a quilt, and faced towards the reflection-less river. The day idled away as he drifted in and out of a feverish, dream-filled sleep.

When there was no improvement the following day, in either the weather or his health, Anwar grew a little concerned, as one; he had a full schedule arranged for the next day and two; he had not yet registered with a doctor.

167

Oh well, he thought – just have to wait and see what tomorrow brings. At least the weather forecast for the following day looked more promising, and a viral fever should only last around forty-eight hours before one could expect to begin to feel somewhat better.

Anwar opened his eyes and stretched. It was very early but he had certainly had a better night's sleep. In fact, the aches and fever of the previous day had all but disappeared. He got out of bed and padded over to the large window. He'd never drawn blinds at night, preferring to be woken by the dawning of the day. The faint salmon-pink tinge of impending sunlight danced teasingly on the surface of the Thames. He smiled. What a relief! And he was even hungry!

After a quick shower he lingered at the breakfast bar, watching the wakening city. Noting the early morning joggers in Potters Fields Park he resolved to begin a fitness regime as soon as he felt fully well. He would join them! After all, he had always been an early bird and had never found it difficult to exercise at dawn. He remained where he sat for a further thirty minutes, mesmerized by the movement of the river traffic and enjoying the confident reign of the eastern sky as it claimed back ownership over the night.

*

A bitter, north wind stiffened his fingers even through his cashmere-lined gloves as he battled to keep his umbrella from blowing inside out. If he were not mistaken, Dr. Karesh seemed to raise an eyebrow as he entered the exam room. But then it was his first visit to the practice. Over the past two months Anwar's feverish episodes had recurred three more times and he was growing increasingly concerned. Whilst the fever symptoms remained present for no more than forty-eight hours, the accompanying aches and pains and muscle tenderness seemed to last progressively longer until, over the past two weeks, he had felt as though he were never free of pain. So much for his resolution to take up morning jogging! The stiffness he experienced upon waking had of late made him feel at least two decades older.

'How long have you been residing in the U.K?' the doctor asked.

'Close on three months,' Anwar answered, having already filled him in on his symptoms.

An unreadable *Mmm* was followed by a cursory examination of Anwar's flexibility in the pelvis, knees and shoulders. 'I'll take your blood pressure – just for our records.' The doctor seemed to be running on autopilot and as far as Anwar could see had shown little concern over his symptoms. 'I'll give you something stronger than paracetamol. See how it goes and come back if things don't improve. I'm sure it's nothing to worry about – probably just your body's way of adapting to its new environment.' He scribbled out the prescription without looking at Anwar, tore it from the pad and stood up. Although not entirely satisfied, Anwar felt obliged to leave. He muttered his thanks and hurried back outside, the weaker opponent against the persistent gale.

It was so frustrating! Anwar was so passionate about his work at the university, and his teaching gave him such a sense of purpose, that the fact that his body was letting him down became more and more exasperating with each new ache. Apart from a few, mysteriously pain-free days over the Christmas holidays, Anwar was, by the middle of January, rarely out of pain.

A second visit to the Medical Practice, this time to see a different doctor, was met with a rather more thorough response.

'Your symptoms *could* signify the onset of rheumatoid arthritis.' She peered at him over her reading glasses as he re-tied his shoe laces.

Anwar frowned.

Seeing his look of concern she back-pedalled somewhat. 'No need to worry just yet. Let's do a blood test and take it from there. In the meantime, we'll try a non-steroidal anti-inflammatory. It won't do any harm and will hopefully ease your symptoms.'

The previous prescription had made him feel nauseous and hadn't eased the pain in the slightest so, after two days, Anwar had stopped taking the pills and had instead reverted to his usual paracetamol. He would give these a try though, as his joints certainly felt inflammatory. Sometimes even the skin on the affected areas would become reddened. He could literally feel the heat caused by the inflammation.

Anwar had just finished leading an important seminar with student visitors from Finland when his mobile rang. The previous night had been particularly bad. Throughout, he had tossed and turned, unable to find a position in which he could feel comfortable. When he had got out of bed this morning, his right leg had threatened to give way beneath him. It had frightened him and had certainly put a blight on the seminar... and he had so looked forward to it.

He had stayed behind afterwards and made himself available to take questions from the enthusiastic audience, yet having already stood for over an hour, he was desperate to rest his throbbing legs. Why, even his right thumb had pulsated with pain every time he had switched the presentation slides!

'Is this Professor Hussain? It's Doctor Bartek's secretary.' Anwar was thankful that just a few seconds earlier the final student had vacated the lecture theatre. 'The results of your blood tests are back and Doctor would like to see you,' she continued in what he was certain was a feigned tone of dis-concern.

His heart beat quickened and he heard himself inhale sharply. He hoped the secretary on the other end of the line wouldn't be able to sense his anxiety; after all, he was supposed to be a professional scientist, someone who should remain in control, at least until any diagnosis had been confirmed.

'How soon can I come?' he heard himself ask.

'We have an appointment for six p.m. tomorrow if that's suitable,' she replied.

Anwar was, in a sense, relieved. At least now he should have an answer as to why his once-fit body was letting him down so badly of late. He had always enjoyed exercise. Indeed, he had found it a great stress reliever over the years of high-pressured study, but this constant pain made him feel old. He was sure he looked older too as lately, every time he caught his reflection, he was met with a frown of agony.

'Well... it's good news and bad news,' Doctor Bartek said, before he had even had chance to sit down. But then again even the motion of going from a standing position to a sitting one seemed to take a while these days. Your blood tests show that you are extremely deficient in Vitamin D. In fact, I have never seen anyone with such low results. This strongly suggests that you have a condition called osteomalacia – an adult form of rickets. There... that's the bad news over.'

Anwar smiled. A sense of relief that nothing more sinister had been found washed over him; why, at that moment he even imagined his aches seemed a little less acute!

'Now for the good news... The condition is totally treatable with a high-dose Vitamin D supplement. I do suggest though that you also try to include foods high in

171

Vitamin D in your diet. I'm sure you know what they are,' she smiled. 'And you might also want to try a light box, especially on gloomy days, or days when you are too busy to spend time outdoors.'

Anwar exhaled loudly through his nostrils, as if until now his breath had been baited. All this suffering caused by something as simple as that! 'Do you know, it's strange,' he began, suddenly feeling the urge to talk. 'I remember thinking during my flight here that I may not get to experience sunshine too often in London. Little did I know then how much pain it would cause.' He beamed with genuine relief.

Doctor Bartek returned his smile. 'I'd like you to make another appointment for two months time, just to check that your blood levels are improving. And be patient! It may take some time for symptoms to really improve and for the inflammation in your joints to calm down. There should be no long term damage though.'

Anwar couldn't wait to begin treatment. He considered himself blessed that the solution to his ailment was such a simple one. Of course he would read into the condition a little more widely, in order to ensure that he was doing everything he could to give himself the best chance of complete cure, but the diagnosis really was a huge weight off his mind.

Anwar had made it through February and was certain that things were improving. He had modified his diet to include fortified breakfast cereal, more eggs, fish and cheese and had also switched to soy milk.

He had also made every effort to spend at least a half hour a day outdoors, but the time of year really hadn't helped at all. It was so cold that any attempt to absorb sunlight naturally through his skin was thwarted by the layers of clothing he needed to wear in order to bear the temperatures. The photo-therapy from using the light box seemed to help though – at least with the anxiety and depression which went hand in hand with his physical symptoms.

The inflammation had not yet subsided sufficiently to allow him to take up jogging but he had begun a gentle, daily work out at home in order to prevent his joints from stiffening further. And in any case, hadn't the doctor warned him that it was likely to be some time before the inflammation completely subsided? All in all, he felt that things looked more promising.

Hence it was with great disappointment that he was recalled to the surgery at the end of March only to be told that his levels of Vitamin D had plummeted even further. And he'd been so sure his symptoms were beginning to improve! This time, the doctor had looked more concerned, and had referred Anwar to a specialist for further tests. He already knew from his own research that there could be several reasons why his body was failing to absorb the Vitamin D but had put the possibility of the supplements failing to the back of his mind.

There would be two further months of waiting and worrying, and at a time when all he really wanted to do was immerse himself in his work and focus on helping to advance the next big potential in the quantum computing world.

As part of a world-wide programme his professorship at the university was partly sponsored by Microsoft. This meant that the university's academic research labs could be used in order to help move from pure theoretical physics towards engineering with the building of qubits. It was very exciting times in the world of quantum computing and Anwar was so thrilled to have been granted the opportunity to be part of what was current. It also meant that he had several international trips to make over the coming months, including one to Austria, where their physicists were taking a leading role in such development and then another to California. He could most certainly do without falling seriously ill now!

Further blood tests, an M.R.I. scan and a thorough examination by the specialist all proved inconclusive. Apart from further depletion in his Vitamin D level and his obvious physical pain, which by now had worsened to the point where even simple everyday tasks had become burdensome, there was absolutely no indicator of any specific disease to be found in Anwar's body.

In some ways this was comforting, and yet at the same time, having no specific answer as to why he was constantly in so much pain, was extremely vexing. However, within two days of being immersed in the bright skies Austria had to offer, Anwar's symptoms seemed to improve again until, by the end of the week, he felt almost back to his normal self. For the first time in several months he began to hope that this period of suffering might be coming to an end.

Unfortunately, just three days after returning to the sombre skies of London, his symptoms once again reared their ugly heads. In fact, if anything, the pain and stiffness had worsened until it had become an inauspicious presence. Since this last recurrence he had found it necessary to use a cane to help him walk, and despite continuing to take the pills, as well as carry out all the non-prescriptive measures that he could, Anwar's condition continued to deteriorate. The specialists were just as baffled and talked about carrying out conductive nerve tests as the next step.

Anwar had of course carried out his own research into his symptoms, but despite his wealth of scientific understanding, he felt as though he were simply being led round and round in circles. Until the worsening of his condition following his return from Austria he had not wanted to admit to himself the possibility of a soma-significant cause; but now he had to acknowledge that this was distinctly plausible.

Could it really be that his love of the sun and subsequent lack of it in London during winter was actually the cause of his ailments? If that were true then how could the severe depletion of Vitamin D, despite his taking the supplement, be explained? Was it possible for such a quantifiable indicator to be effected solely by the mind? The maddening thing was, that before these symptoms had appeared, he hadn't felt at all depressed and hadn't even noticed the gloomy weather– at least not consciously. It really was only his constant pain that had led to him feel depressed. After all, wouldn't anyone whose life was suddenly turned upside down, during what should have been such an exciting time, feel the same?

Of course he was aware of Seasonal Affective Disorder and its symptoms, but what he had gone through these past months was surely far more serious than that. Yet if the specialists, despite all their tests, could find nothing amiss then he began to think his condition had to be caused by his own mind.

Anwar had for some time been fascinated by the notion of quantum super-positions and had studied the work of renowned physicists who spoke on such theories. Just like these quantum physicists, Anwar too was somewhat reluctant to give credence to the mystics of quantum physics and the mind, and yet at the same time he had to acknowledge the suggestions that the mind could genuinely affect the outcome of measurements. Was it possible to conclude then, that his mental state might in itself affect the lack of absorption of Vitamin D?

*

By now it was late May and the weather had improved

175

somewhat. However, periods of high pressure, and thus more sunshine, were insufficiently long enough for Anwar to be certain as to what effect, if any, they were having over his symptoms. There were just *good days* and *bad days,* typical of any inflammatory disease, and so Anwar's hope of full recovery began to diminish.

If it hadn't been for his job he thought he would simply have packed his bags and returned to Saudi. But his genuine fervour for his work managed to sustain him. It would be just two weeks until he and Yan would pay a second visit to California, and this time they had tagged some vacation days on to the end of the trip so that they could enjoy the sights.

*

Glacier Point, Yosemite Park! It was somewhere Anwar had always longed to visit. Apart from his work he also had a passion for star-gazing, and doubted there was anywhere finer in all of America where this could be enjoyed. He and Yan had made a reservation to spend three nights at Upper Pines camp-site, and on the third and final night had also arranged to join a local star-gazing club so that they would have access to professional telescope facilities. He hoped and prayed that the skies would be clear.

His disability meant that Yan had needed to help him carry his camera equipment during the final climb to the peak, but all in all, he was feeling better than he had done for the past few months. His spirits had soared during the course of the trip. Witnessing the cutting-edge research being carried out at Pasadena Institute of Technology had been tremendously exciting, and what with the university also having one of the world's best departments of Astrophysics, Anwar had begun to re-discover his former self. In fact, he had been so completely immersed in the experience that he had finally managed to put his aches and pains to

176

the back of his mind. They were still there of course, but he was sure they had eased substantially. Whether this was down to the prevalence of sunshine or purely down to his happier state of mind though was anyone's guess.

Exhausted by the climb, Anwar lay on the rocks, snug in his sleeping bag, and merely observed the magnificence of the sky for the first thirty minutes or so. The amphitheatre at Glacier Point provided unobstructed views of the heavens. The thinnest sliver of a waxing crescent moon allowed him to view the Milky Way even with the naked eye.

By 10:30p.m., the moon was no longer visible, and so, with the aperture of the telescope carefully aligned, Anwar watched mesmerized as one gaseous nebula after another came into view from beyond Earth's solar system. The compatible camaraderie of the group, along with the spectacular performance of the night sky, began to make him feel whole again.

As the night progressed Anwar grew physically tired. He lay snuggled in his sleeping bag, as close to the edge of Glacier Point as he dared. Despite the rapidly plummeting temperature, he felt warm. Binoculars in hand, once again he simply watched...

Tonight's stargazing felt different from that of previous occasions. Tonight wasn't a night for scientifically analysing and measuring what he saw; it was a night for offering up his mind to the majesty of the skies; a night for allowing himself to simply become part of what was, in fact, a portal to infinity!

He did not want this night to end. He felt lighter than he had for such a long time– less burdened. The longer he watched, the more a part of the whole spectacle he became...

We are just atoms within atoms he thought. Under his

breath, he hummed the tune to Moby's *We Are All Made of Stars,* smiling at the lyrics. Its message was simple; Anwar had never even considered it before, but tonight, simple or not, it conveyed how he felt.

As his mind drifted, he became distantly aware of movement and chatter amongst his fellow stargazers.

'Time to go buddy!' Yan stood, beaming down at him. 'It's past 3:00a.m. We're all freezing! Let's go get some sleep.'

Anwar yawned, yet he was not tired. He had not felt so relaxed, so at one with himself and the universe for such a long time. He wasn't cold at all! 'You go ahead Yan. I'm staying put. I want to see the sun rise.'

Yan hesitated, wondering whether or not to try to persuade Anwar to return to the camp with them; after all, he had been so unwell of late. But all said and done he was an adult and should therefore be allowed to make up his own mind. 'You sure? I'd stay with you, only I'm desperately tired all of a sudden and so cold!'

'Absolutely certain,' Anwar said with a grin. 'I doubt I'll ever have this opportunity in my lifetime again.' He stood, without pain, in order to say goodnight and convey his sincere gratitude to the group.

'Well, if you're sure buddy.' The group leader shrugged. 'We'll leave the telescope set up. You'll be able to use it and it'll save us from trying to dismantle it in the dark. You can come back down with us when we return in the morning.'

'Great! I'll take great care of it, don't you worry.'

He watched them leave in the dark, the faint beam from their red flash-lights growing dimmer and dimmer...

He stretched, then huddled back down onto the rock. He did not feel even the slightest sense of loneliness; how could he when he had so much company in the skies?

Truth be told he was grateful for the solitude now, for as much as he had enjoyed the company of the others, his mind had turned a corner. He no longer felt afraid of what the future might hold for him. With only the stars for company, he felt more confident and at peace than he could ever remember...

And oh how he longed to watch the sunrise from this transcendental spot on Earth!

*

Anwar must have inadvertently drifted to sleep, for he was suddenly woken by the cold. Upon opening his eyes he saw that apart from the stars, which continued to watch over him, the sky remained pitch-black. He climbed out of his sleeping bag and instead wrapped it around his shoulders. Glancing at his watch, he saw that it was about an hour to sunrise. He returned to the telescope...

The brightest point in the sky heralded the king of the gods – Jupiter. Its tawny-white cloud belts hugged its generous middle whilst its great, red spot seemed to fix intently on Anwar. They had connected, this gargantuan planet and this speck of a man! Anwar watched as its four largest moons tip-toed timidly around their master. He was sure he could almost feel the pull of its magnetic field willing him to join in praise of it.

The Mighty Jupiter laughed in the face of the comparatively tiny pawn that was Mars. Anwar's insides flipped with excitement at the prospect of witnessing the breaking of dawn, for he knew that it would not be long before it arrived. For all the excitement that was the sky at night it was the dawn that Anwar craved now. He sat again, on the edge of the rock, and watched... and waited... patiently.

Nautical dawn. Anwar knew that the sun had reached an angle of twelve degrees below the horizon. The sunlight reflected by Earth's atmosphere was now sufficient for him to just make out the peaks of the Sierra Nevada against the sky. He watched transfixed, knowing that in front of him, tumbled the might of Yosemite Falls. What a spectacle it should make once twilight truly held the reins!

As the selective scattering of sunlight coruscated over the falls, the torrent turned swiftly from blush to crimson, before reflection and refraction conspired to create a rainbow which danced wildly as the water spilled over the mountain. Anwar's whole being was filled with joy. Eyes moistened, he knelt on the ground and gave praise.

As he raised his head, he saw that the whole sky was filled with the brightest light. No! Not just the sky but the Earth too! It was the light of a thousand photons! He stood with ease - unaided and unafraid - and blinked into the distance...

Nothing but an auspicious stream of light illuminating the path ahead!

Anwar stepped towards it.

Bunker

During the night of 12th of December 1940, the City of Sheffield and it's surrounding areas were targeted by the Germans in what became known as The Sheffield Blitz. Great damage, particularly to the city centre occurred, and there was substantial loss of life.

A second wave of bombing followed on December 15th.

The following story is a work of fiction based on these events...

December 12th 1940, North East Sheffield

For a few moments the high pitched whine of the soprano sax drowned the siren, but reality soon dawned.

'Quick Ethel! Let's go!'

The girls linked arms, giggling as they scurried towards the dance hall's exit, the humid heat of the throng pushing and shoving all around them. The cold, damp chill of December night air hit the second they stepped outside.

'He was! Really he was!' Ethel was certain that at the moment the siren had sounded the love of her life, Billy Reed, had been strutting his way towards her to request a Lindy-Hop. She had longed for this moment for ages and now, just as her dream was about to be realized, it had all been ruined by those fecking Germans!

'Well if he's that keen he'll ask again next Saturday!' Joan was not at all convinced that a dance with Ethel had been Billy's intention. Why Ethel was so batty about him she could not understand! She melted like butter in his presence, becoming all soft – not like her at all! 'I don't

183

want to be a misery Eth,' but you could do better. He's no good! Look at the way he treats his mam! Bleeds her dry he does. My father always said, "If you want to find out if a man's worth anything, just look at the way he treats his mother."'

Ethel groaned. 'He's not that bad Joanie! Just doesn't earn enough to stretch 'til pay-day that's all; and besides, those brooding brown eyes!' She shuddered with pleasure and gripped Joan's arm tighter. 'And in any case, he's soon to turn eighteen. Probably about to get called up the way this bloody war's going! Got to grab my chance while I can haven't I.'

In kitten heels, they stumbled along the pitch-black street towards the public shelter in the disused railway tunnel known as *Fiery Jack*. Breathless and half-drunk on the thrill of the dance-hall they reached the entrance.

'Me bloody hair's all frizzy now!' Ethel moaned.

Reaching inside her purse, Joan pulled out a red polka dot headscarf. 'Here, tie this round your head. You don't want Billy mistaking you for his pet poodle do you? Might offer you a bone!' The pair erupted into hysteria.

'Now, now! Calm down ladies.' Peter Collins was the A.R.P. on duty and you didn't want to mess with him. He was a real stickler for the rules. 'We need everyone calm and collected down here remember,' he said, taking in every last detail of the girls' somewhat dishevelled appearance in one swift glance. 'Does your mother know you're out this late Miss Pierce?' His disapproving frown spoke volumes.

Joan stopped giggling instantly. Her excited expression melted to one of innocence. 'Yes of course Mr Collins. She lets me go to the dance on Saturdays now that I've turned seventeen; knows I'm safe with Ethel here.' She nudged Ethel, who was still giggling, hard in the ribs. It was alright for her – her mam let her do whatever she wanted as long as she tipped up her pay packet from the factory each Friday. But as for her own mother – well, she was a different kettle of fish altogether.

The shelter was filling up. So many people out on the town of a Saturday night meant plenty caught out in the event of an air raid. Joan watched Peter Collins grow more and more frazzled in his efforts to control the merry-makers, the majority of whom had just vacated the same dance hall as the girls. Ethel stood on tip-toe, straining her neck, her attention obviously elsewhere.

'Stop bloody looking for him!' Joan pulled her deeper into the shelter, away from the door which was soon to be closed by the warden. In the distance, a screaming wail, quickly followed by an explosion, caused the girls to duck instinctively. 'Sounds like the city's taking a beating,' said Joan turning pale.

They squeezed themselves into a space on a wooden bench and gazed around at their fellow inmates. 'Ah well,' Ethel sighed, reaching into her purse to touch up her lippie. 'S'ppose I'll just have to wait another week then.'

The crowd, many of whom were at least a little tipsy, were already joined in song.

> 'Kiss me goodnight, Sergeant-Major,
> Tuck me in my little wooden bed.
> We all love you, Sergeant-Major,
> When we hear you bawling, "Show a leg!"'

Without hesitation Ethel joined in, any dismay over her imagined missed opportunity with Billy already forgotten in the camaraderie of the crowd.

Joan leaned her back against the cool, damp wall of the tunnel and observed the scene. She remembered a year back, to the first few times the sirens had sounded. It had been a very different experience then; everyone full of fear but trying to keep it together so as not to frighten the children. Now, they had become almost blasé. After all, whilst other parts of the country had taken major hits during the raids, so far they had experienced no serious damage closer to home. Her thoughts sobered quickly. Was it right she wondered? Was it right to sing and dance and go out to clubs when elsewhere so many lives were being lost?

She was soon jolted back to the present though, as Ethel grabbed her hand and swung it in time to the tune. 'Cheer up Joanie! You look as though you've seen a ghost! For God's sake!'

Joan smiled and made a feigned attempt to join in, but being far more of an introvert than Ethel, she found it difficult to make an exhibitionist of herself. Sometimes she wished she wouldn't think so much – just let herself go with the flow a bit more. But she was too much like her father – at least that's what her mother always said. And she supposed it was true. And what was more, she was proud to be like him, for if ever there had been a good man it was him; the best father and husband anyone could have wished for...

It had been four years now since they'd lost him but she still missed him terribly.

*

It had been one of the worst nights he'd ever known. Sheffield had taken its first big hit of the war and Collins had been run off his feet all night. Still, damage to this part of town was nothing compared to the city centre. By all accounts it was on its knees. In his neck of the woods they'd had a lucky escape with just a few casualties. Apart from the roof of the cinema being blown off and a few incendiaries dropped, there'd only been the bombing of the viaduct. They'd managed to get everyone out of the cinema alive but the viaduct – well, they'd not been quite so lucky there.

He was all in! Weary to the bone!

It was almost 4:30 in the morning before the all clear could finally be sounded. Now he would just need to clear out the occupants from the shelter, most of whom he assumed were probably sound asleep given the fact that the majority of them had been pretty inebriated when the raid had begun. He tutted to himself disapprovingly and shook his head. Still, he did not relish what was to come; after all, he would have to deliver the news that some of them no longer had homes to go to,   and worse still for those who lived in the city centre, for news had already spread that serious damage and loss of life had occurred there. He'd start by giving them the good news though, to *soften the blow* so to speak.

*

'What do you mean they're all gone?' Anger resonated down the line in the Chief Warden's voice.

What did he think Collins was doing? Playing silly buggers? After the night he'd just had that was hardly likely! Still, he found himself repeating what he'd already said, 'Yes Sir– They're all gone. I know it sounds impossible but it's a fact – there's not a soul inside. I need help. I can't for the life of me begin to think what's happened.'

'Well man, how long did it take you to return to the shelter after the all clear?'

Collins understood the enormity of wrath the chief must be feeling given the whooping Sheffield had just suffered, but there was no point in taking it out on him! He inhaled, attempting to quell his frustration before answering. 'No more than a minute or two Sir.'

'That's hardly bloody likely now is it,' the chief spat down the line. 'They must have left by the emergency exit. Either that or you took a damned sight longer than two minutes to get back there and they'd already buggered off. Think logically man! They can't have just disappeared into thin air now can they!'

Collins held the receiver away from his ear in order to lessen the impact of the chief's bellow. 'Now we're bloody busy here! It's been a bad night you know! A real bad night! Make some enquiries around town and get back to me if you must.' The receiver was slammed down hard, leaving Collins shaking with both fear and temper.

There was no other exit. He was certain about that. Just he and Wilfred Taylor supervised this part of town. Perhaps Taylor had beaten him to it and had already overseen the vacation, but he knew that was not the case. Still, he supposed Taylor should be his first port of call – if only he could find him.

Taylor stood at his front door in vest and trousers. 'You pulling my leg?' His unshaven face paled as Collins delivered the news. Collins knew that he too had not had a wink of sleep all night. Even though he was supposed to have been off duty he had turned out to help. Why, he'd only taken his leave of him about half hour earlier. Taylor had said he was off to his sister's to break the news that their aunt's house had been flattened. 'Rather she heard it from me,' he'd said. Right now Collins was glad that Taylor'd returned home first as he had no idea where his sister lived.

'For pity's sake Taylor! What do you take me for? They're gone I tell you! Each and every one of them!'

One look at Collins' ashen face was enough to reassure Taylor that the man was indeed telling the truth. 'Hold on. I'll grab my coat,' he said, already retreating down the narrow hallway.

Both men marched in step along the dimly lit street. Dawn had not yet broken and blackout still reigned. In the distance, a smoking orange glow from the fires raging in the city centre lit the sky, enabling them to navigate their way more easily along the streets. Most houses were pitch-dark, their occupants having returned to their beds after a sleepless night. Collins' heart thumped loud in his chest and he dug his hands deep in his pockets to hide the fact that they were shaking. He had a real bad feeling about this – a *real* bad feeling!

'How many d'you reckon were inside?' Taylor asked as they drew close.

'About two hundred or so – usual Saturday night crowd; most of them worse for wear. Raucous lot to be honest.' Collins looked down at his feet, somewhat embarrassed by his obvious inability to tolerate the foolish. He was aware that Taylor rather enjoyed a tipple and hoped he didn't consider him stuffy. 'Where on earth can they have got to?' he continued. 'If I find out someone's playing a blinder, I swear I'll have them locked up. This is no laughing matter!'

'Course not Pete. Surely no-one'd play a joke like that, 'specially not after the night we've just had.'

As they turned the corner, the door to the shelter came in to view. Just a few paces further... Collins hesitated, suddenly reluctant to go back inside.

'Here, let me– ' Taylor shouldered the door heavily, then, without hesitation, stepped inside.

The silence was a chasm. 'They can't have been gone long,' Taylor whispered, though quite why he found it necessary to do so he wasn't sure. 'It's still warm in here – and the smell!'

Collins inhaled deeply. Taylor was right. The usual musty, damp scent was tainted with the malodour of stale, breathy ale. He ran his hands through his lank hair. It seemed like a dream. He sighed with exhaustion, longing to go home and get some kip.

Their torches cast a beam along the length of the tunnel which sloped away gently into the distance. Dust motes danced mockingly in the air; the only life to speak of the fact that this place had recently been occupied. The lamps had all been extinguished which was strange. Together they set about re-lighting them. A warm, ochre glow cast sepia shadows along the walls, encouraging calcite deposits on the roof to twinkle menacingly, as though the answer to the mystery might be found within their crystals.

'You never said they'd left their belongings!' Taylor's mouth was agape as he stared about him.

How had he not noticed? A row of overcoats stood pegged, just inside the entrance. Those topped by a fedora or cap appeared particularly forlorn as they awaited their owners' return. And there – there on the bench – a red polka-dot headscarf lay strewn, its garish print screaming for attention amidst the drabness. Handbags, umbrellas and the odd briefcase leaned patiently, waiting to be re-claimed. Atop one of the bunks, a much-loved teddy pleaded with sorrowful eyes for an answer. A wash of acidic bile rose in Collins' throat, its bitter taste complimenting his suspicions. 'I... I didn't notice. It was too dark.'

Without speaking, they strode the length of the tunnel. Collins' old knee injury protested at the downward gradient, which ended abruptly in front of a bricked wall. Funny, he'd never really noticed the slope before. But then he had been on his feet non-stop for the last ten hours and his leg was certainly giving him gyp. The dank, silvery surface of the tunnel walls glistened in the beam of his torch.

'Jesus Christ Collins!' Taylor suddenly gasped and covered his mouth with his hand. 'What's that bloody smell?'

Collins winced at the flippant manner in which Taylor

had taken the Lord's name in vain. No reprimand ensued though. He sniffed the air. 'Sulphur – Yes it's definitely sulphur.'

'Perhaps they've all been poisoned!'

Collins realised Taylor was not thinking rashly which was out of character for him. 'Don't be daft lad! There'd be bodies.'

'Jesus Collins! I'm losing my bloody mind! Course there would!'

Collins grimaced a second time.

Taylor took several deep breaths in an attempt to calm himself. 'Right then, let's think logical here. If you're certain you got here more or less immediately after the all clear, then the only possible conclusion is that for some reason they must've all decided to take their leave beforehand.' Despite the churning in the pit of his stomach, Taylor was trying hard to keep it together. 'Think hard Pete. Try to remember who was 'ere last night. If we 'ave names then we can start by trying to find out if they've made it home. You never know, perhaps some Tom Fool decided to make his way home in the middle of the raid and returned with some story that encouraged the rest of 'um to follow suit.'

Collins stood puzzled, head in hands. 'Joan Pierce– Yes! She was definitely here with a friend of hers– What's her name?' He bit his bottom lip hard. 'I can't remember! But I know Joan well – nice family.'

'You know where she lives?'

'Yes, yes, not far – Mill Road.'

*

'No, she's not come home! I'm worried sick!' Elizabeth Pierce wrung her hands in agitation as the two men stood on her doorstep.

Collins sighed deeply. He couldn't help but somehow feel responsible for what had happened.

191

'I've been round to Ethel's already. Her mother's not heard from them either; doesn't seem too concerned though. But I know my Joan – she would never worry me like this, always comes straight home she does.' She blew her nose loudly in her handkerchief and Collins noted the raw, red flesh of her hands. A wave of pity engulfed him. He knew that Mrs Pierce had had to take any work she could find after the untimely death of her husband; such a nice family they'd been too. And what about Joan? Her father had had high hopes of sending her to college but those had fallen by the wayside after he'd gone. He swallowed hard, wondering if poor Mrs Collins might have lost Joan too. If so, it would be too much for her to take.

'Try not to worry Mrs Pierce. I'm sure they'll turn up soon. We'll come round straight away, soon as there's any news. I promise.'

*

'This simply cannot get out man! Do you understand? What would it do for public morale?' The chief spluttered, red in the face with fury.

Both Collins and Taylor were worried sick. A whole day and night had passed since the discovery of the empty shelter and now the townies were outside, hammering on the tunnel door demanding answers. Why! Taylor was even sure the press were outside. Bloody vultures! You'd think they'd have had enough blood to bathe in, given the devastation in the city, without needing to peck round 'ere.

Since the second phone call to the chief, both Collins and Taylor had been ordered to remain in attendance at the shelter. Once the boss had rolled up, they'd been imprisoned inside. He'd brought a couple of high and mighty civil defence agents with him and they'd quickly fixed a bolt on the door from the inside to keep out the mob.

'But you have to tell them the truth! How are you going to explain the fact that they won't even have a body to bury if you don't?' Collins was trembling as he addressed the chief.

The chief only glared at him harder. 'We have our ways of alleviating the public's fears! Don't you worry about that. It won't be your responsibility to come up with a plausible story.'

Both men had heard the whispers. A certain *expert* on missing persons was apparently on his way, a Professor Bartholomew Brockett. He sounded important; so important in fact that they were prepared to wait for him to come all the way from Devon. Collins hoped the professor would realize the insanity of the situation and do something to calm the crowd.

'What the hell Pete? There has to be a logical answer to this somewhere.' Taylor searched Pete's desperate face in the dim light, as if the answer might somehow be revealed there. What on earth did the boss think he was doing? This was crazy! Over two hundred people disappear into thin air and this bunch were not willing to let the truth be told! He'd heard of cover-ups before but this was on a whole new scale!

Collins' empty stomach lurched as a hard, firm knock reverberated at the door. Finally! This had to be the professor. Why! His very knock sounded on the mettle.

Collins glanced towards the entrance, as the agent guarding the door threw the bolt. After twenty four hours of darkness, the sudden shaft of sunlight hurt his eyes. He squinted in its direction, anxious to see who was there.

A tall, authoritative figure, immaculately dressed in a dark-grey civilian suit, stood with his back to them, calmly facing the crowd. His rather abundant head of hair - the colour of ripe corn - appeared to brandish a halo in the sudden bright light. The crowd lurched, fingers pointed and voices raised. The merest hand gesture and a genuine smile from the gentleman however, easily subdued them. To Collins' amazement, the frenzied town-folk appeared to have fallen under his spell.

His voice had a smooth, silvery tone when he spoke. 'I promise that we will have answers for you very soon; but in the meantime I kindly ask that you bear with us,' was all he said before stepping into the gloom of the shelter. The bolt was swiftly drawn behind him and the crowd could once again be heard to take up their rant with ardent fervour.

Collins glanced at Taylor in an attempt to ascertain whether or not he too considered what had just come to pass as strange. Taylor's top lip, now bearing a five o'clock shadow, glistened with sweat. His pallor reminded Collins of butcher's tripe.

'Bartholomew Brockett. Pleased to meet you.' A steady hand was held out for Collins to shake. In doing so, he locked eyes with the professor. He truly believed that you could tell a lot about a person by looking into their eyes. Doing so provided only a brief opportunity for judgement, but this man was kosher – he was certain. His nerves calmed and for the first time he realized he had eaten nothing for a day and a half. The rumbling of his empty stomach echoed in the depths of the tunnel. He flushed red, glad of the dimness.

Having been filled in on the details of the previous night, Bartholomew Brockett requested to examine the length of the shelter for himself. Both Taylor and Collins stood up from the low bench, intending to lead the way. They were quickly dismissed however, by the chief instructing them to remain where they were.

Both men strained their ears in order to listen to what was being said as the bunch of civil defence agents slowly made their way along the entire length of tunnel. The acoustics of the place helped to carry the words in their direction. There seemed to be much focus on the professor's part on the presence of the sulphurous smell.

A considerable length of time seemed to be spent examining the brick wall at the rear of the tunnel. The waiting men, now out of earshot, grew increasingly frustrated. 'Damn it Pete, I'm ravenous! How much longer they gonna keep us down 'ere?'

'Your guess is as good as mine,' Collins muttered dispiritedly, stretching his aching back against the cool wall.

Eventually the men returned. Even in the gloom of the tunnel, Collins could plainly see that the chief was ashen. For a few moments, nothing was said. The agents shuffled on their feet in apparent discomfort. Both Collins and Taylor stared hard at them, expectantly.

It was the chief who eventually spoke, and for once his tone towards the men was civil. 'Now I realize you've had an exhausting twenty-four hours or so and are probably keen to go home, freshen up and get some food down you, but we have one last favour to ask of you both.' He attempted a smile but instead of putting Collins at ease, the look of insincerity in his eyes only served to make him more nervous. He glanced at Taylor who also appeared unconvinced.

'Professor Brockett has suggested that we need to get a specialist team down here, to further examine the wall at the rear of the tunnel. Now, we would be most grateful if you two chaps wouldn't mind sitting it out for a bit longer, until we can rally the right men– ' He paused, half expecting the two men to protest. 'We'll see to it that hot water and a good meal is brought to you as soon as we clear the mob– Of course, we'll need to put a lock on the outside,' he said, glancing shiftily at Collins, 'for your own safety. After all, we don't want you getting mobbed by the crowd.'

Collins watched him wring his hands and understood how desperate he was. 'You have my assurance that your ordeal will soon be over. We should have you out of here once and for all by tomorrow evening at the latest.' His small, current eyes, almost lost within the ample folds of his face, darted from one to the other as he spoke.

'But Sir! We're done in!' It was Taylor who spoke, but before he could protest any further, the chief once again took up the cause.

'We really can't afford for what's happened here to get spread about you understand. You know how folk are– a rumour here, a tidbit of gossip there and before you know it the whole damn town's alight!'

'But Sir– What has actually happened?' It was Collins' turn now. Against his nature though it was to question authority, this whole thing was fast becoming a charade. There were no answers! At least none that he had been made aware of.

The chief's face reddened again. He cleared his throat loudly, asserting his authority. 'Now, now Collins! Let's not get above our station and start asking too many questions. The professor has a good idea as to what might have happened here, but it's not within my remit to provide you with those answers just yet.' He glared at Collins, daring him to push further, all too aware that it was not in the man's nature to do so.

He had won. Collins felt himself suddenly deflate. The physical exhaustion and mental anguish of the last day and night had him beat. He slumped back down upon the bench. Taylor pitied him but he too had nothing left. 'I'll stay if you will Pete,' he said, his own voice little more than a whisper.

Promises of good food were reiterated as the team of agents hastily gathered their belongings. Just as they were about to take their leave, Bartholomew Brockett spoke.

'May I thank you both sincerely. What we have asked of you goes above and beyond the call of duty.'

Collins was certain he could detect genuine sorrow in his eyes. His kind words softened the blow and a lump threatened to form in Collins' throat. The professor turned to take his leave, but before reaching the door took a step back. 'Just one last thing men– Whatever you hear out there, don't let it worry you. Sometimes the truth has to be amended a little in order to appease those who would not understand.' And with that, the whole team stepped out into the noisy throng, leaving Taylor and Collins alone again.

'Well lad! Looks like we're here for the duration,' Taylor said, attempting to lighten the mood.

'Shush Wilf! Let's listen to what they're saying out there.'

The sound of the chief's orotund tone penetrated with ease through the door. 'I'm afraid it's not good news,' he began. The crowd instantly hushed, a few soft cries of dashed hopes breaking the silence. 'It appears as though the nearby explosions have caused the rear end of the tunnel to collapse.' Taylor frowned towards Collins and shook his head.

The distraught cries grew more audible now, the voices peppered with clanging sounds as a lock was fitted to the door. The chief allowed them a moment to absorb what they had just been told before continuing. 'Now we realize that many of you might wish to stay – probably even volunteer to help. However, we need to bring in a highly specialist team in order to secure the place and search for any survivors. As the tunnel stretches a fair distance below ground, we will therefore be cordoning off a wide area here. We request that you remain in your homes whilst our work is carried out.' Not a hint of deceit or betrayal in his voice.

'Jesus Christ Pete! Can you believe it? What a pack of

bloody lies!' Taylor was on his feet.

'Hush man! Let's hear what else he has to say!' Collins' heart beat fast in his chest.

'There's plenty of miners here who can help! Let's get on with it,' someone bellowed from the crowd, only to be swiftly hushed again by the chief.

'We appreciate your concern, but I assure you this is no ordinary cave-in. Without the specialism of the team, who are already on their way to assist, there will likely be further collapse. Your frustration is understandable. However, we must insist that you now clear the area and allow the work to begin.' This time, the composed, silvery tone of the professor's voice seemed to do the trick, for within seconds, no more than a few murmurs of protest could be heard amongst the crowd. 'We give you our word that it is the only possible way of us finding any of your loved ones alive and returning them to you safely,' he continued. 'Now– return to your homes. You must all be exhausted.'

Gradually, the crowd could be heard vacating the scene.

'God Almighty Pete! I think we've been taken for fools here,' Taylor said, obviously shaken. 'Nothing but a rotten pack of lies!'

Collins did not reply. He was more afraid than he had ever been in his entire life.

December 16th, 1940, North East Sheffield

Elizabeth Pierce's cup rattled as she attempted to replace it on its saucer. Arms cradling her middle, she stifled a moan as the officer delivered the news that all attempts to find missing persons had been called off. Rocking in her chair, and sobbing inconsolably, she failed to take in anything more that was said.

'You mean they're all gone?' her neighbour Mrs Booth asked, herself also trembling with shock.

'I'm afraid so. Last night's bombing put pay to the whole rescue attempt. Sadly, the area above the shelter took a direct hit. It's been razed to the ground.' He paused. Yanking at the front of his uniform jacket, in a feigned attempt to straighten it, he got to his feet. 'May I offer my sincere commiserations Mrs Pierce. I'm so sorry that nothing more could be done.'

Irene Booth showed the officer to the door. After he'd gone, she stood and leaned her back against it, sighing deeply. She had no idea how Elizabeth would come to terms with this news. She had clung on to a thread of hope, but now... Joan had been her two eyes. Wringing her hands, she headed back to the kitchen.

*

East End Sheffield, August 1943

Professor Brockett's hands trembled ever so slightly as he turned the key in the heavy gauge lock and heaved open the weighty, anodized gate. Re-entering the Austin 12, he proceeded slowly, before again exiting the vehicle in order to secure the gate behind him.

Cautiously, he proceeded towards Gate 2, noting as he did so how nature had been quick to claim its stake on the land for already the second track was barely visible – and it had only been a few years.

'You know, I still struggle on a daily basis to come to terms with what we had to do,' he sighed. 'Those poor men.'

The SIS Officer accompanying him had only to meet his eyes for the briefest of moments to establish that his words were spoken with sincerity. He shrugged. 'Simple fact is Brockett, that unfortunately there are times when the lives of the minority must be sacrificed in order to ensure the survival of the majority.'

Having parked up, they solemnly approached the

entrance to the building, then paused in silence, as though beside a grave. Upon entry Brockett closed the main door softly, as though afraid to disturb the nothingness inside, before locking it behind them. Another door, just a few paces along a featureless corridor, led to a small, grey room marked **Office**.

The silence inside the building was tangible. It seemed as though the air itself had been awaiting their arrival.

Brockett held his breath, before flicking a row of switches along the far wall. The machinery whirred to life, sending a plethora of dust motes into excited animation. Both men watched in trepidation as the dials climbed slowly from red to green. Brockett exhaled loudly, expelling the last degree of tension. Just fifteen minutes in which to check the rest of the building before they would need to shut the apparatus down again and re-secure the compound.

'They've done a good job here,' the SIS Officer said, his torch tracking the outline of the solid steel door poised at the far end of the corridor. 'Nowt'll get through that.'

A cold rush of air molecules, expelled from the SIS Officer's nose as he spoke, blew against Brockett's skin, causing him to shiver.

Inspection complete, the men silently retraced their footsteps along the gradient ahead.

Two top-quality woollen suits in charcoal grey, camouflaged against their surroundings.

Just a hundred paces.

And if it hadn't been for the crowning halo of corn-coloured hair worn by the man on the left, **Door** would hardly have known they were there...

Acknowledgements

So many people, in so many ways, have helped my writing journey, often without them even realising it: the children I taught, my friends, my family. I thank you all.

Tony, I say this every time, but without your inspiration and ideas this book would not exist. For the listening, the superb artwork and animations, as well as all the formatting, thank you. I will love you forever and a day.

To my mother, who is no longer with us, for all her encouragement and story-telling during my childhood years, I am so grateful.

To my father, for his lifelong patience and belief in me – I love you.

A special mention goes out to friends and colleagues, past and present, who have supported me by reading and reviewing my books, and especially Elaine Murphy and the 'Costa Ladies Wot Read' book club for their kind words and reviews of my previous work.

Last, but certainly not least, I would like to thank my readers for choosing this book in the first place. I hope you enjoy – and remember – I cannot be held responsible for any bad dreams you have as a result of reading!

A writer's best friend is a reviewer. If possible, please spare a few moments to leave your thoughts on Amazon or Goodreads.

Thank you.

About the author

Catherine McCarthy grew up in the industrial valleys of South Wales where she went on to teach for almost three decades.

She is the author of The Gatekeeper's Apprentice — a fantasy adventure for middle grade readers, and Hope Cottage — a dark and mysterious family saga for adults.

Door and Other Twisted Tales is her third publication.

She is currently engrossed in writing a magical realism novel, set in mystical West Wales, where she now lives with her husband, who is also her illustrator and motivator.

Catherine believes that story telling is probably the oldest and wisest art form known to man, though to make it compelling, it needs to be crafted with a bit of magic.

For more information and examples of artwork and illustrations please visit...

https://www.facebook.com/authorcatherinemccarthy/

Printed in Poland
by Amazon Fulfillment
Poland Sp. z o.o., Wrocław

53203283R00125